Martin Millar was born in Scotland and now lives in London. He is the author of such novels as *Lonely Werewolf Girl*, *Curse of the Wolf Girl* and *The Good Fairies of New York*. Under the pseudonym of Martin Scott, he, as the *Guardian* put it, 'invented a new genre: pulp fantasy noir'. *Thraxas*, the first book in his Thraxas series, won the World Fantasy Award in 2000. As Martin Millar and as Martin Scott, he has been widely translated.

Visit Martin's website at www.martinmillar.com
www.facebook.com/martin.millar
www.twitter.com/MartinMillar1

Praise for *Martin Millar*:

'The funniest writer in Britain today'
GQ

'Martin Millar writes like Kurt Vonnegut
might have written, if he'd been born fifty years
later in a different country and hung around with
entirely the wrong sort of people'
Neil Gaiman

'Imagine Kurt Vonnegut reading Marvel Comics with
The Clash thrashing in the background. For the deceptively
simple poetry of the everyday, nobody does it better'
List

'The master of urban angst'
i-D Magazine

RUBY
AND THE
STONE AGE
DIET

MARTIN MILLAR

piatkus

PIATKUS

First published in the UK in 1989 by Fourth Estate
First published in the US in 2010 by Soft Skull Press
This paperback edition published in 2012 by Piatkus

A CIP catalogue record for this book
is available from the British Library.

ISBN 978-0-7499-5782-7

Typeset in Bembo by M Rules
Printed and bound by CPI Group (UK) Ltd, Croydon, CR0 4YY

Papers used by Piatkus are from well-managed forests
and other responsible sources.

MIX
Paper from
responsible sources
FSC® C104740
www.fsc.org

Piatkus
An imprint of
Little, Brown Book Group
100 Victoria Embankment
London EC4Y 0DY

An Hachette UK Company
www.hachette.co.uk

www.piatkus.co.uk

LIVING IN BATTERSEA I one day arrived home in the early morning and found a corpse, it was the body of a girl who has been around for a short while, I didn't really know her. She spent her time with the heroin users up the road.

Outside my squat there is a little garden with scrubby grass. She is dead in the scrubby grass.

Never having seen a corpse I wonder if they are really stiff. I poke her skin and it is indeed stiff, and very cold.

She has some mess around her lips like vomit. She is very young.

Finding the corpse perplexes me. It is not a normal experience and I am unsure what to think.

'A dead body,' I say.

'Yes,' agrees Ruby.

Ruby is my friend. We squat together in an Army Careers Office. She never wears any shoes.

We stare at the corpse and at that moment it starts to rain.

'Look,' says Ruby. Two small raindrops have fallen right under the dead girl's eyes.

'Raindrops like tears,' says Ruby. 'It is hugely symbolic.'

MARTIN MILLAR

I feel some relief. Everything is all right once Ruby names it.

Minds at rest, we go inside and wait for someone else to find her so they can call the police.

'What it needs now,' says Ruby, 'is for the radio to play "*You're Sixteen, You're Beautiful, and You're Mine.*"'

'Yes,' I agree. 'If that was to happen it would be immensely poignant.'

But when I switch on the radio the only station we can find is broadcasting a report from the Tokyo stock market instead, and no matter how we try we cannot work this up into any really effective kind of imagery.

I try humming it, but it's not the same.

Some years later, Cis wants some flowers. I'm pleased. Now I can go and get something for her.

She wouldn't mind if I didn't. She doesn't even expect me to get them. She just mentions that it would be nice to have some flowers around the house.

I leave the flat and walk round the corner, searching. I find a flower stall. It has appeared by magic.

I have never bought flowers before. I try and imply this, looking vacantly at the paper-wrapped bundles.

The young woman doesn't mind me being vague, and I buy some daffodils.

'Here, Cis, I brought you some flowers.'

She smiles. She wasn't expecting them. I said I was going out for cigarettes. I bought cigarettes as well.

Cis is very happy with the daffodils. She smiles more and finds an old glass vase and puts them in water and puts the vase on the table and kisses me for bringing them.

I am deliriously happy. Nothing could make me any happier. I love Cis. I could not love anyone any more than I love Cis. I will go to any lengths to bring her flowers.

Later I tell Ruby all about it.

'Cis said they were lovely flowers,' I say, and Ruby tells me it was a good thing to do. She says there is nothing wrong with a bit of romance, even in a world where poor people have to sleep in cardboard boxes and young girls sick themselves to death on heroin.

One time I am walking home a long way after a party in North London. I have no money for the bus and possibly there is no bus, so I walk and walk. Halfway home I start to feel feverish and it comes on so rapidly that just a street or two after I first notice it I am sweating and tiring and my throat is starting to swell.

The pavement is strewn with crushed glass. It sparkles under the streetlamps. The notion enters my head that it is a design put there for me to enjoy and I say thank you for making such a pleasing design to entertain me when I am walking feverish along the pavement.

In the centre of town where the night buses start I beg money for a long time. I am too tired to walk all the way home. I'm hot inside, hot, feverish, drunk and drugged. Finally I raise the bus fare.

At home I wake up with some virulent flu germ and I lie in my one room for a long time in a flood of sweat and self-pity and dream about the rain. My muscles hurt and my joints ache, particularly my knees, which won't support me to the sink so I have to be sick on the bedclothes.

I am sick for a week and no one visits and if I died then no one would find me till maybe the landlord thought it was time to rent out the room again.

The fever rages. After a week I feel better and go out to buy a book to get me through. In the bookshop the assistant is wearing two long silver earrings with opals in them. The opals catch the light and it reminds me of the sparkling pavement.

Back in my room I make a cup of tea and read one page of the book when the fever starts to rage worse than before and I can't read or even finish my tea. I lie on my own for more days and wonder where you find a doctor if you don't have one, but I'm too sick to find out.

The fever makes me shake and shake and I hallucinate slightly. I wonder why no one visits and I feel lonely and one day I am so lonely I start to cry.

After a while I recover. It was a bad illness but when I tell people about it later I can't impress on them how sick and lonely I felt, though as it turns out that lying sick and lonely in a room somewhere with no one visiting is not such an uncommon experience; perhaps they know anyway.

I wake up in the morning with Cis wrapped around me, still asleep.

I look at her closed eyes and think about what we did last night, which was mainly nothing, watching television, making food.

Cis is a bad cook. So am I. We don't worry about it. We ate our bad food and looked at the flowers, then went to bed and made love.

This morning I am perfectly happy.

Cis gets up. I watch her getting dressed and rummaging her hair into position. Her hair is bleached white and cut into a flat top, but Cis is so beautiful it doesn't really matter what she does with her hair, or anything else. Cis is the sort of girl you see for five seconds in the street then think about once a week for the rest of your life.

Hair finished, she has to go and visit her mother. I go back to sleep, thinking how good it is to wake up with someone you love wrapped around you. I am still perfectly happy. I am happier than I have ever been before.

Ruby and I are living in a council flat. We have shared many different places to live and we get on very well. When I get home the whole place is a shambles and she tells me she had some friends round for a few drinks the night before.

'How is Cis?' she asks, always willing to make pleasant conversation. 'And can you help me with my hair?'

I help her with her hair.

'Cis is wonderful,' I say happily, and she sneers a little, but pleasantly.

She tells me what good acid she had last night with the few friends and drinks and I say it sounds nice but really I am not keen on acid because I tend to get strong and unpleasant hallucinations.

'Have you found a drummer for your band yet?'

'We're auditioning some tonight,' I tell her.

'Look. I cut my foot.'

'You should wear shoes.'

'I hate shoes.'

Ruby is always barefoot which is practically unique in the city. The only things she ever wears are a lilac cotton dress that comes down to just below her knees and a pair of sunglasses. She wears nothing under the dress and nothing over it, except a donkey jacket if it is cold.

With her dress, bare feet and sunglasses, she looks wonderful.

A broken bottle has proved too much even for her toughened soles. I bring a basin of water and wash her feet, then stick a plaster over the cut.

'Thank you,' says Ruby.

★

Cis comes round. I bound around the flat trying to do things for her. She gives me a potted plant and tells me she doesn't want to see me anymore. I think I might die on the spot.

Ruby wanders in and offers us some tea. 'Yes, thank you.'

'Why don't you want to see me anymore?'

There doesn't seem to be any particular reason for it.

Ruby brings the tea and Cis goes away. I look at my potted plant. It is a little cactus.

'Will you go and cash my Giro for me?' asks Ruby and signs the back.

I go to the Post Office. It is robbed. I am surprised at this. Normally it is a quiet place. Robbers come in with machine-guns and hold me and all the other customers at gunpoint and demand a small jet to fly them to Libya. All the hostages shake with fear.

The siege lasts for hours and hours till finally specially trained police burst in and shoot all the robbers dead. There is blood everywhere, blood and television cameras.

I cash our Giros and go home.

'Ruby, I'm sorry I was so long cashing our Giros but when I was in the Post Office robbers with machine-guns came in and held me hostage.'

Ruby says don't be silly and I say it is true and she says it is just the acid making me think funny things and I say what acid and she says the acid she put in my tea to make me feel better about Cis leaving me and after that I can't think of anything good to say.

'I wrote a werewolf story while you were out,' says Ruby. 'Do you want to hear it?'

'Yes.'

'Then sit down comfortably.'

Cynthia Werewolf – her early life

Cynthia, a good but hungry werewolf, always tries her best not to eat people. Sometimes, however, it is an uphill struggle. They taste nice.

An outcast from society, she lives alone with her mother. They do not get on very well. Cynthia is always lonely.

At school she has no friends. The other children do not know that she is a werewolf, but they can sense she is different.

Every full moon Cynthia has an unbearable urge to eat someone. This, however, is absolutely forbidden by her mother.

'Under no circumstances are you to eat a human being,' her mother instructs her sternly.

'Not even a little baby that no one would miss?' pleads Cynthia.

'Particularly not a little baby. Babies are absolutely not on the menu as far as we are concerned. And nor is anybody else.'

Cynthia, never very happy, annoys her mother, who tells her continually that she has a lot to be thankful for.

'Outside it is a beautiful world.'
Hungry and lonely, Cynthia can't see it herself.

~

I get a job for three days on a building site in Wandsworth. It is meant to be for longer than three days but the foreman tells me not to come back because I am not much use.

I am a little hurt because I have been trying my best but I know that it is true. I can manage clearing rubble in wheelbarrows, although I am not very strong, but when it comes to levelling out wet concrete with a sort of vibrating machine I am hopeless.

I often do this sort of temporary work when I am broke. It is the only work I can get.

On my last day a man in my shift tells a joke.

Everyone laughs. I am still waiting for the joke to end. I seem to have missed a bit. I will have to ask Ruby to explain it to me.

But Ruby is not home so I go to my room and feel bad about being sacked after only three days. If I had been able to practise a bit more I'm sure I could have worked the concrete-levelling machine.

Outside my window a nice-looking boy walks past. He is just the sort of boy that Cis would like. He might even be her new boyfriend. He might be going to see her right now. The thought of Cis with a new boyfriend is too terrible to contemplate.

I would like to phone Cis but I know she doesn't want to hear from me.

Where I am standing everything becomes unbearable. I walk to the other side of the room to see if it is any better there.

No success. This side of the room is just as bad.

I figure maybe I should do something to take my mind off Cis. I will tidy the flat.

My room has cobwebs in the corners but when I think about how to clean them away it seems to be an awful difficult thing to do and maybe not worth the trouble as they are sure to come back in a while.

Ruby must be across in the next block with her boyfriend Domino. I wish she was here to talk to.

I don't like Domino. Ruby is very smart. He is dumb.

Ruby is writing a book. Domino can hardly read.

Outside the window is a pathetic little window-box with a dead weed and five cigarette ends. I think about planting some flowers in it then taking them to Cis. Looking out the window I see her go past. I walk back to the other side of the room but nothing has changed there.

The next day I am captured by a spaceship. It swoops down on me when I am walking through Trafalgar Square and takes me away for some tests. The aliens look quite normal but I am worried they might be wearing masks and underneath they are really horrible and scaly. Still, I am not one of these people who is totally paranoid about space aliens. After all, there is no real reason for them to be unfriendly.

So I try and co-operate the best I can with their tests and after a while, when I have taught them some English, we get on quite well and they show me round. Their spaceship is full of luxuriant flowers, all lilac and yellow and bursting with life. They try bringing me some tea as they read in my thoughts that I am very fond of tea but the machine that makes it gets it a little wrong. Still, I appreciate the thought.

Ruby arrives back. I go for a talk with her but she is busy writing a letter.

'Who are you writing to?'

'I'm writing to my genitals.'

I borrow her book of myths and fables and sit beside her, reading.

'Where do you want to go now?' asks the Captain of the space aliens.

'Just back to Trafalgar Square,' I say, and they drop me off.

I wander round for a while thinking about the aliens and wondering if I should tell anyone about it but just down the road at Charing Cross I lose concentration when I suffer a dreadful hallucination that there are rows and rows of people living in cardboard boxes, so I hurry on past and catch the bus back to Brixton. It is raining and this makes my knee hurt and I wish I had remembered to ask the space aliens if they could cure it, because my knee is often sore.

Back on Earth I start missing Cis again. I cannot think of any reason that she would have left me. Disappointingly, Ruby is unable to explain the joke the man told on the building site.

I show her the potted plant that Cis gave me as a leaving present. Two tears dribble from my eyes.

'Never mind,' says Ruby. 'At least it is a nice cactus.'

Afreet, says Ruby's book, *is the evil God of Broken Relationships. If you offend him your lover will leave you.*

'I met Izzy today,' says Ruby. 'She is having terrible problems with her boyfriend and she has bought two weights to build up her body.'

'What sort of weights?'

'Little ones. She wanted something bigger but the woman in the shop told her that she had to start off small. Apparently it is the repetition that counts. Her boyfriend is secretly fucking someone else.'

I would like to phone Cis but I know she doesn't want to hear from me.

Cynthia eats the first of many victims, or the first one that is discovered

Cynthia and her mother live on a small croft in the Scottish Highlands. They live alone. A few years ago her father left the family. He ran off with a younger werewolf.

Cynthia's mother insists that her daughter should go to university. In the modern world werewolves always try to integrate themselves with society. Cynthia is not keen. She wants to go and sing in a rock band and play her guitar loud.

One day she is out for a walk through the heather. She comes across a pregnant woman.

Aha, thinks Cynthia. A nourishing sandwich. And there's no one around. She eats the pregnant woman. Unfortunately her mother, sharp-eyed, is not as far away as she thinks, and sees the crime.

Her mother is furious. So is the Werewolf King. Cynthia is forced to flee to London with only her guitar for company.

~

I can never find a reliable drummer for my band. This is on my mind while I am patching my jeans and feeling hungry. My jeans are a shambles and we can't afford any food.

'I think we should become Buddhists,' says Ruby.

'I am busy patching my jeans.'

'See? You are too concerned with the material world. Once we are Buddhists you won't worry about patching your jeans or stuff like that.'

'Are you religious about your drumming?' I once asked a drummer, in a shabby all-night café in Soho.

'Not really. There is no god of drumming. But I do follow the way of the Tao.'

'What will Domino say if you became a Buddhist? Will you still be able to fuck him?'

'Domino can fuck himself,' says Ruby.

They have been arguing again. I think about Ruby's suggestion.

'If I become a Buddhist will I stop being sad about Cis?'

'Right away.'

Next day, in heavy rain and very hungry, we go up into town to join a Buddhist temple.

They give us a vegetarian meal which tastes very good and we sit around banging tambourines for a while. I pretend I am banging a tambourine in tribute to the God of Drumming so he will send my band a good drummer.

'I am enjoying this,' I say to Ruby, and she seems quite enthusiastic as well.

Everyone has shaven heads and we wonder if we will have to have this done. Ruby says she doesn't mind, even though she has lots of meticulously cared-for hair, because spiritual people don't bother about this sort of thing. Also we will get nice orange robes.

After we've banged our tambourines and chanted and had some more vegetarian food a man comes and sits with us.

'I am your instructor,' he says.

'How long have you been a Buddhist?' asks Ruby.

'We're not Buddhists,' says the man. 'We're Hare Krishna.'

We pick up our shoes on the way out.

'What a disappointment,' says Ruby.

'How come we picked the wrong temple?'

'At least it was nice food.'

'The act of eating disgusts me,' says Ruby. 'Do you think I am putting on weight?'

'No.'

Ruby worries about her weight. It is stupid. She is not overweight.

A string of shaven-haired devotees marches past, chanting and banging drums.

'Don't ask them to join your band,' advises Ruby. 'You'll be wasting your time.'

'Is that—'

'No it isn't. Cis isn't here. And it doesn't look anything like her.'

'Why did you write a letter to your genitals?'

'I was just telling them how much I dislike them. It is a procedure recommended in my new book. Next I have to write them another letter telling them how much I like them.'

On the way home we meet Izzy who is eating a pizza in the street and carrying a small weight.

'I have to screw this onto my dumbbells,' she tells us. 'It's time to make them slightly heavier.'

She is wearing a leather waistcoat. She flexes her bicep.

'Do you notice any difference?'

Ruby and I say yes although actually we don't.

'How are you getting on with Dean?' asks Ruby. Dean is Izzy's boyfriend.

Izzy shrugs. There is a definite kind of shrug that means you are not getting on too well with your boyfriend.

Back home I go through to look at my cactus.

Ruby follows me into my room.

'Let me have a look at that cactus.'

She studies it for a while.

'This is sensational.'

'What?'

'This cactus. According to my book of myths and fables it is the sacred Aphrodite Cactus. Once it flowers your love is sealed forever with the person that gave it to you.'

'When will it flower?'

'Any time.'

It is February. Any time cannot be far away. I am pleased to have Aphrodite on my side.

Cynthia is very poor, but meets a pleasant companion

In London Cynthia squats with a few people she meets around. She is very poor. The Social Security will not give her any money and she is forced to scavenge the streets to survive. She tries mainly just to eat dogs and cats, because she does realise that it is not such a nice thing to eat humans, but sometimes she devours one. Humans are very tasty.

And, when she thinks about it, humans have never been all that pleasant to wolves, and they do eat animals themselves.

Still, after eating a human Cynthia always feels a little guilty. But when she meets a nice boy called Daniel and starts going out with him she soon forgets all about it, because Daniel is a friendly lover and they both like to fuck for hours on end.

Afterwards they watch television or listen to records, and Cynthia plays Daniel a few simple songs on her guitar.

~

Ruby comes back from Domino's, slamming the door, holding a cactus and forcing a smile.

'Domino bought me a sacred Aphrodite Cactus. I made him do it. He wanted to spend the money on beer instead. Look after it till it flowers.' She storms off, apparently unhappy despite the cactus.

I put it next to mine and feed them both some plant food. Outside it is thundering and lightning and lashing down rain.

One time around midnight I met a girl called Anastasia at a bus stop in the rain at Clapham Common. This sticks in my mind because Anastasia is an unusual name. No buses came so we started walking together. At this time I was still in the Army Careers Office.

'It would be nice to control the weather,' said Anastasia, pulling her collar tight against the rain. 'Like a rain god. I'd walk around in sunshine all day long. Maybe I might have a little bit of rain so I could make some rainbows.'

I go through to Ruby's room and ask her what is wrong and she says that Domino is a complete moron who wants to drink beer all the time and he reminds her of her father.

I try being sympathetic but I am not a very convincing liar and Ruby sees through me. We disappear into our separate rooms and I get back to staring at my potted plant. I had considered writing a poem but now I don't feel much like it because with Ruby in such a bad mood I will have no one to show it to. But this is probably just as well, because I am a terrible poet.

It rained till the gutters overflowed onto the pavements. At the corner of Battersea High Street Anastasia quoted me three lines of a poem by Byron and told me she would like to come home with me. This was a surprise, but fine.

Possibly I am massively attractive that night. Possibly she is dreadfully lonely. Probably she is just fed up with getting rained on.

At my front door I find I have lost the keys.

'I have lost the keys.'

We look at the front door. It is barricaded like a good squat should be, with a rough sketch of Tilka, Guardian Goddess of Squatters, protecting the entrance. Hammering on it produces no results. No one is home.

'Never mind,' I say. 'I'll get in the back.'

I walk round the corner and beat on Paul's door to let me in and then I climb his back wall and walk through the gardens of some rented houses and avoid a barking dog to clamber into our backyard. I force the window at the back of my room. Once inside I can't get out because I now remember I have padlocked my room on the outside as a security measure against everyone else who squats there.

So I have to hop out the back and break the window of the next room. Unfortunately once inside the room I find that the person who lives there has followed my example and this door too is padlocked outside.

I curse him for being so suspicious of his fellow human beings and wonder what to do. By this time I am growling with frustration and Anastasia is somewhere outside in the rain wondering where I am, so I just take hold of the door and beat it till the locks break. The door is in shreds.

I run to the front door and haul it open.

'Hi Anastasia, come in.'

We enter my room via my neighbour's room, the back-yard and my window.

Up above spaceships fly through the night sky, puny human craft and mighty alien movable worlds. Somewhere on a mighty alien movable world two beings are clamber-ing through a window and into bed. Being mighty aliens they will have conquered all sexual diseases and will be able to fuck with complete abandon.

'This is an interesting way to get into bed,' says Anastasia, clambering over the window-ledge. After undressing she takes a diaphragm from her bag, smears it with spermicide, and pushes it into her vagina.

After fucking I have the longest journey ever up to the kitchen to make some tea and carry the teapot back through the obstacle course of the shattered door. Two windows and a backyard is no easy matter. Later I have to make the same journey again to rummage round for some dog-ends to roll a few cigarettes, but all in all it is a pleasant experience, though as I never see Anastasia again, possibly she does not enjoy it as much as me.

The following day Danny in the next room is furious that someone has torn his door off its hinges but I just deny all knowledge of it, and when he gets round to taking some glue and some heroin he soon forgets all about it.

Cynthia gives way to her appetite

'Let's go out for a walk in the beautiful full moon,' suggests Daniel.

'No,' says Cynthia. 'It's not safe outside at night.'

'Don't be silly,' says Daniel. 'Of course it's safe.'

Round the first quiet corner Cynthia changes into wolf-form, kills Daniel and eats him. The full moon always gives her a powerful appetite.

'I told you it wasn't safe,' she says.

Daniel did have the slightly unfortunate habit of often not listening to Cynthia's opinions carefully enough.

~

Ruby comes out of her room and starts being friendly. I immediately co-operate because if Ruby is friendly to me I will always be friendly right back, even if she has been unpleasant to me only minutes before.

'Here is some tea,' she says. 'Help me with my hair.'

She is tying some small lilac ribbons into her plaited locks.

'They are lovely,' I tell her. 'They look beautiful with your dress.'

'I'd like to show them off. Let's go out.'

We walk down into the centre of Brixton and call on Izzy. Izzy lives with Marilyn. They are both Ruby's friends rather than mine. Marilyn is not in and Izzy is busy lifting her weights. They seem like very small weights but she must have been lifting them for a while because her body is glistening with sweat.

'See the improvement?' she says flexing her biceps.

'Yes,' we say, although neither Ruby nor I can see any difference.

Izzy is wearing a dull yellow tracksuit with the sleeves ripped off and holes in the knees. For some reason I feel sorry for her, standing there in rags, pretending her muscles are growing.

Before we go Ruby asks her how she is getting on with Dean. Izzy tells us she is mad at him because he is busy rebuilding an old motorbike and never has any time for her. And then when he does call round he expects her to drop everything and pay him lots of attention. What's worse, she always does. And she still thinks he is fucking someone else.

We leave Izzy to her weights. Outside Ruby says she feels a little sorry for her, though she isn't sure why.

We set off again to visit some more of Ruby's friends.

When we arrive they are busy putting some padlocks on their front door.

'Can't be too careful,' says Phil, who is a small-time cocaine dealer, and attracted to Ruby.

When they hear about how Domino has been unpleasant to Ruby and I have been left by Cis they do their best to cheer us up.

'How could Domino be so unpleasant to you?' says Phil. 'Compared to him you are a goddess.'

Later on I go home and Ruby stays. Close to our flat I am so full of things to cheer me up that I find myself lying face down in a puddle with a vivid memory of someone telling me that you can drown in only two inches of water.

I struggle to my knees. Only an inch and a half, I estimate. A lucky escape. Four young men pass by, singing and shouting and causing a disturbance. I hate them. They ask me if I am all right and they go to a lot of trouble to help me home. I still hate them.

Next morning I wake up in bed with the Great Goddess Astarte.

I am surprised, of course, that the Great Goddess Astarte has chosen to visit a council flat in Brixton, let alone sleep in my bed, but I go along with it because I do not want to offend her in any way. I have nothing but respect for the Great Goddess.

At this time I am working for a man in Dulwich who does painting and decorating. I have to strip off wallpaper with a steaming machine. It is unpleasant and difficult.

Some people do easy jobs and earn huge amounts of money. I do dreadful jobs and am always poorly paid. I am not quite sure why this is. Maybe I didn't pay enough attention at school.

When I am doing these menial things I think about whatever band I'm playing in at the time. I imagine us being successful. I imagine that one day I will not have to visit any more building sites or factories because I will be making records and making money and having fun. Even though I am realistic enough to know that this is unlikely, I still think about it.

However, I abandon the decorating because I cannot leave the Great Goddess to go and strip wallpaper. It would be a terrible insult.

For some days I go around making food and keeping the flat tidy and generally being organised because I am sure that the Great Goddess will be totally fucked off if she keeps tripping over old clothes on the floor or finds there isn't any soap in the bathroom.

She seems to adjust to the modern world very well, working the TV doesn't cause her any problems at all and she consistently plays all the best records in Ruby's and my collection. Ruby seems to be away somewhere, which is a shame as I know she would have liked to meet Astarte.

'Can you make Cis come back to me?' I ask, respectfully bringing her a cup of tea.

'Of course,' she replies. 'I can do anything. But I'm not going to. She has a life of her own to lead.'

'Oh.'

I think about asking her to find me a good drummer but I do not want to burden such an important being with my petty problems. She has told me that she is presently engaged in trying to stop the world being destroyed by heartless humans. Apparently it is a very close thing. She does however take the time to say a few words to my cactus and afterwards it is always spectacularly healthy. It starts to grow, but there is no sign of a flower.

Cynthia finds happiness with another lover

After eating Daniel Cynthia is very very lonely. She deeply regrets it. So she takes her guitar and goes busking in tube stations to try and earn some money and take her mind off things.

She is quite successful at busking. Cynthia has a good voice. Also, something about her eyes makes the police hesitant about moving her on.

Later, still lonely, she has a drink in a pub.

A girl comes over and talks to her. Her name is Albinia. They go home together.

Cynthia moves in with her and they are happy for a while. Albinia is a dress designer and works every day in a studio surrounded by other young artists who she finds very pushy. She appreciates Cynthia's relatively simple manners, and she likes her singing.

Cynthia, of course, does not let on that she is really a

werewolf. She knows that Albinia will find this hard to understand.

~

I meet a man who can't relate to the world because he is too shy to talk to anyone. He is too shy to talk to me and we don't have any fun. I meet a woman who hates herself because she is fat and she apologises for not saying she was fat in the contact advert. I tell her not to worry about it because I don't mind but she says she knows I am lying and that really I hate her for being fat and she wishes she'd never met me. I meet a man of fifty who runs a company making yachts and he says he is looking for a nice young houseboy who he can fuck on his own personal yacht but I am not good-looking enough so it isn't going to be me. I meet a man who lives in a cardboard box under the National Theatre and he promises that he is only living there whilst pursuing a sociological study of the homeless and if I will take him home and let him fuck me we will be very happy together. I get rained on and wet waiting for a woman who wants a young lover to take her to art galleries and she never shows. I meet a young man with a withered arm who says he used to be a drummer until he got burnt in a fire. I like him but he says he never wants to have sex because he is ashamed of his withered arm and he is sorry he wasted my time. I brush my hair downstairs in McDonald's whilst waiting for a young soldier who promises he has books, magazines and videos, but he never shows and I don't wait long because four noisy young men at the next table are making me nervous. I meet a man who wants to teach me to fly helicopters but when we get undressed he is nervous that I will steal his suit so he cannot concentrate. I meet a woman who says she is embarrassed about placing an advert but since her husband died she has not been able to stop crying and the doctor told her to get out of the house more. I meet a young woman from Iceland who is so bright, intelligent and attractive that it seems like a bad miracle that she cannot meet anyone she likes and has to sit every night alone in a bedsit with one ring of her gas cooker lit because her electric heater is too expensive. On reflection she decides that she does not want to sit there with me. I do not want to sit there with her. I do not want to do anything with anyone. I want to wake up in bed with Cis.

I wake up in bed with Ruby.

'Good morning, Ruby. Where have you been? Why are you in my bed? Where is the Great Goddess Astarte?'

Ruby tells me to stop rambling and says she will make us some tea. I rush out of bed to make the tea myself.

While the kettle is boiling I have to go and be sick in the toilet and while I am sicking up a little blood I try and think what has been happening the last few days. However, with the vomiting and the kettle boiling over and Ruby screaming will I bring her a bit of toast as well I can't get much thinking done so I abandon the attempt.

I wonder what day it is.

'What day is it?' says Ruby.

Neither of us have any idea.

In the mirror I look like a corpse. I am sorry the Great Goddess has gone but pleased Ruby has come back. After a while, when I don't feel like vomiting anymore, I walk round to the shops for some cigarettes and a bar of chocolate for Ruby. When I'm there I look at a newspaper to find out the date and I find it is Saturday, which is in some ways a pity as we both should have signed on at the Unemployment Office on Wednesday and forgetting to sign on is practically the worst thing you can do when you are on the dole.

On the way back I think that I see Cis coming towards me with a dog, but when the person gets up close she is nothing at all like Cis, she is an old woman of eighty with a carrier bag containing her week's shopping and I can see from the way she carries her shopping that she is the loneliest person in the world. Probably all she has to talk to is a cactus.

'Here's your chocolate, Ruby.'

Ruby looks distressed and says she does not want any chocolate as chocolate disgusts her.

'But you asked me to buy it.'

'How are the potted plants coming along?'

'Very well. I think mine's grown with all the food I've given it. If Cis was to come back right now she'd be really pleased how well I've looked after it. No flowers though. Are you sure you don't want this chocolate?'

'Yes. What do you know about diaphragms?'

'I know what they are.'

Ruby is surprised. She does not really expect me to know anything.

'I am having trouble with mine.'

I make her some tea and Ruby tells me how lonely she feels when Domino is not around, and how good she feels when he brings her little gifts like bars of chocolate.

Ruby is the most intelligent person I know and also very strong. Why she is bothered by a fool like Domino not being around to bring her chocolate I can't imagine.

Cynthia suffers a series of misfortunes, and thinks of home

'Isn't it nice,' says Albinia, 'the way that our periods have started to coincide since we started living together.'

'Yes,' says Cynthia, the scent of blood in her nostrils.

The full moon shines through the window.

Cynthia eats Albinia.

The neighbours hear screaming and break down the door. Cynthia is forced to flee.

She finds a rubbish tip and lies down to cry.

I am cursed in love, she thinks. Why did I do it?

Later that night she suffers further misfortune when the rubbish tip internally combusts and her leg is burned in the fire. She limps off to nurse her wound. Thunder crashes in the sky above and it starts to rain.

Soaked, lonely and injured, Cynthia thinks about her comfortable home far away in Scotland, and her mother.

'I do not think it is a very beautiful world, no matter what you say,' she mutters, and tries to find somewhere dry.

~

Ruby and I are sitting quietly. Sometimes we sit quietly for hours. Domino is incapable of this. He talks continually because he has to hear his own voice all the time. I hate him.

'Look.'

Ruby has made a spaceship out of the chocolate wrapper. We fly it round the room for a while till it is time for me to rehearse with my band. Wrapping my guitar in a black plastic bag I walk down to the studio, but when I arrive only Nigel is there and he says the new drummer we recruited has decided not to play with us after all but to go away for a long holiday in Denmark instead.

'Is it nice in Denmark?'

Nigel doesn't know. I offer him some chocolate but he refuses because not having a drummer makes him too depressed to eat. Also the chocolate is not too appetising after resting wrapperless in my guitar case. He departs in silence and I try and visit some people but no one is in so I have to go home.

The next launch is particularly successful. Crowds cheer ecstatically and in no time at all we are plunging into deep space. I like our spaceship except this time I notice all the daffodils and lilacs are plastic, and I am not at all fond of plastic. Before take-off I strongly request some real daffodils but apparently they are bad for the oxygen supply.

The President radios his congratulations on the successful launch. I complain to him about the plastic daffodils.

'And where is my guitar?' I ask, but he pretends not to hear.

All the crew are busy with scientific experiments. I am busy trying to tidy my little cabin, brushing away a few cobwebs and programming our computer on how to make me a guitar, when suddenly we are bombarded by a ferocious meteor storm.

'Why didn't the computer warn us?' cries the Captain.

'Its memory banks are all full of instructions on how to make a guitar and long love poems about some woman called Cis,' reports the First Mate.

We are battered mercilessly by the meteors. The door to the airlock is ripped to shreds and only heroic action by some crew members prevents total disaster.

Eventually we struggle through. Afterwards no one will speak to me because they are all annoyed at me endangering their lives by jamming up the computers. Fortunately by this time the computer has made me a guitar so I sit on my own in my cabin and work out a few songs and when the person in the next cabin bangs on the wall complaining about the noise I just ignore it. They disturb me by exercising, always banging weights around and doing push-ups.

I become quite friendly with our robot.

Later in the day Ruby appears with Domino and they act like they are the happiest couple in the world. I wait for Cis to appear so we can also act like the happiest couple in the world.

After a few hours it seems like she is not going to call round today. Maybe she is busy. Possibly she will call first thing in the morning. Suddenly it strikes me that if today is Saturday then it is time for me to get round to the art class where I work one day a week as a model.

I get washed. I never like to think that I smell bad when people are painting me.

'Hello,' says the teacher, a woman of about thirty-five with a cultured voice.

'Hello,' say all the students of all ages also with cultured voices. There is a little screen for me to get undressed behind which always strikes me as strange.

I have no real idea why the art class needs someone to get undressed to be their model but if they are willing to pay it is fine with me, also they are always very nice to me and sometimes buy me a drink afterwards. In fact, some-times afterwards they all fall over themselves to talk to me and be pleasant. Possibly they are keen to let me know they do not regard me as being in any way inferior because I have been sitting there for two hours being painted with no clothes on.

Today the teacher puts lots of boxes beside me. I am disappointed. I was hoping for some daffodils. She piles up the boxes a bit like a robot and tells all the students to make their paintings like boxes. Or robots. Or something like that, I am not too clear about it.

Sitting being painted I am very lonely. I talk to Cis in my head.

Only another twenty minutes, I say to her. *Then I'll be finished. What would you like to do tonight?* I get the feeling that it is unbearable where I am and I want to walk to the other side of the room to see if it is any better there, but as the one thing the art class requires of me is that I stay still this is not possible. A pity, because the other side of the room looks like it might be better.

I wonder if I should tell the art class my problems. Probably they would not like being interrupted in their painting. Everyone always concentrates hard at the class. Also I realise that being left unhappy by your lover is such a common experience that everyone would just be bored by it.

Cynthia's uncontrollable appetite brings her to the attention of the Werewolf King

The Werewolf King is called Lupus. He is immensely rich, and lives regally in Kensington. He has business connections all over and rakes in money from sex magazines and private mailing companies.

When he hears reports about Cynthia eating people he is furious. He hates for his werewolves to eat anyone. Lupus is very keen for werewolves to integrate fully with society. Eating people is disastrous for their image.

Lupus is never happy. His wife ran off with a mathematics student from Africa. Since then he has always looked for people or werewolves on whom to take out his anger.

He summons his werewolf detectives.

'Bring Cynthia to me,' he instructs them. 'Preferably alive, although I won't stretch the point.'

They set off on the hunt. It will not take them long to find Cynthia because werewolves are supernaturally good at tracking.

After his agents depart Lupus relaxes with a bottle of wine and a copy of Voltaire's complete works.

~

The goddess responsible for people whose lovers have left them is called Jasmine and she is always very busy. Sometimes she gets out her flaming sword and battles with Afreet the God of Broken Relationships when she sees that he is about to strike. She is hugely compassionate but she has a high failure rate. Her difficult job sometimes makes her turn to drink, and then there are broken hearts everywhere.

At the end of the art class I get dressed and the teacher

brings out some wine. This is not normal but it seems to be a little celebration for something or other and they all drink wine out of paper cups. When the teacher pours some for me she makes a little wine joke and everybody smiles, but as I have no idea whatsoever what the wine joke is about I just look vacant. Later I have the vague notion that I am pretty dumb compared to these artists who can go around making paintings and wine jokes.

Afterwards I have to go to Stepney to meet a violent sadist who advertised for me in a contact magazine. He is terrible to me and after he beats and fucks me I am half-dead and have blood all down my back. I do not approve of violent sex.

'I don't fit in with the art class.'

'You don't have to fit in,' says Ruby. 'You are only the model.'

'Still, I am pretty dumb compared to them. I used to like it better there but since Cis left me I feel stupid. Also I think my soul has gone missing.'

'Yes,' says Ruby. 'That is possible. You could well have lost it.'

'Where could it be?'

But Ruby is too busy reading her giant reference book of myths and fables. This book is an endless source of wonderment.

I shuffle round the flat trying to find a space where I do not feel bad about Cis. I have bought a little yellow cloth to brush the dust off my cactus. After cleaning it I study it closely for any sign of a flower. I wonder if Cis will reappear as soon as it buds or will she wait till the whole flower appears?

It is now March and there is no sign of a flower.

Cynthia has many unpleasant experiences

Cynthia is evicted from her squat.

She tries eating the bailiffs but some policemen arrive and there are too many of them to fight.

Not for the first time she is left homeless, with only her guitar for company.

Where oh where is a young werewolf to find happiness, she asks herself, and can't think of an answer.

Out busking she is run over by a bus. Fortunately werewolves are very tough and she is not seriously injured, but it is still a bad experience.

Later two men try to mug her and take her day's earnings.

Cynthia turns into wolf-form and eats them angrily. She gets back to busking. A policeman moves her on. It starts to rain. Her guitar breaks a string.

Two werewolf detectives appear.

'We've come to arrest you,' they say.

This is a fucking lousy day, thinks the young werewolf. Everyone is against me. I haven't a friend in the world and I've nowhere to live and I've no one to fuck. The only things I feel are hunger and loneliness. This is far from being a beautiful world. It isn't even pleasant.

Hardened by living rough, she kills and eats the detectives without much trouble, but in the process she loses her earnings down a manhole and finds herself penniless even after a hard day's busking.

~

The old woman is still waiting on her balcony. I wish she had someone to talk to. She reminds me of a woman called Sylvia I used to see in Battersea. Sylvia was around sixty and her Spanish accent was too thick for anyone to ever understand what she said. She lived with a man called Victor who had a cleft palate and no one could understand him either. They could understand each other.

No one ever wanted to see them because they were so filthy and shabby and difficult to understand. Sometimes, for companionship, they would hang around with the local Socialist Workers Party and sell papers for them.

No one cared anything about them and no one ever visited although they lived in a squat in a street full of squats. Just them, sick and old, and a horrible sick dog and not a visitor for months and months. I used to wish that someone would go and visit them.

'Did you ever?' asks Ruby.

'No. I could never understand what they were saying.'

It rains outside and the little balcony floods and we have

to bail it out with a bucket and a pot and this is quite fun because we can pretend we are pirates. Ruby would be a good pirate captain, I think, because she would never have to leave the ship and she could just order the crew about all the time.

Ruby goes to lie down after her exertions and I go downstairs where I meet the postman, the woman from the ground floor and Ascanazl, an ancient and powerful Inca spirit who looks after lonely people. He is drying his feathers after the rain. His feathers are magnificent.

I tell him about Cis leaving me. Almost immediately he makes a polite excuse and flies off.

'You are in a sorry state,' says the woman downstairs. 'Even the powerful Inca spirit dedicated to looking after lonely people is bored with your company.'

I ask the postman if he has any letters for us. We hardly ever get letters. Ruby emerges from her room flushed and annoyed.

'Help me with my diaphragm,' she says.

'What sort of help do you need?'

'I can't fit it. I am going to see Domino tonight and I have this diaphragm from a doctor because I don't want to take the pill anymore but I can't get it fitted right.'

Ruby brings out a tube of spermicide and squeezes some onto her finger, then rubs it all over the round piece of plastic.

'I'll have one last try.'

She lifts up her dress and squats on the floor and

37

squeezes the diaphragm in halfway and tries to fit it but somehow she can't. It keeps slipping out.

'Stupid fucking thing,' she rages.

I try and help. Ruby lies on the floor and opens her legs wide and I insert it.

'Make sure it is stationed securely behind the pubic bone.'

Her vagina is slippery from spermicide but when I fit it, it stays inside.

'There,' I say, always pleased to do Ruby a favour.

'It's not right.'

'How not?'

'It's not covering my cervix,' says Ruby, glowering, feeling inside her with her fingers. 'Do you have any cigarettes?'

I light some cigarettes although this takes several tries as the matchbox also becomes slippery with spermicide.

'Are you sure?'

'Of course I'm sure. Don't you think I know when my cervix is covered?'

She takes my hand and puts my fingers up her vagina.

'See?'

'Not really.'

'Why not?'

'Well, I'm not really sure what a cervix is.'

'You must know what a cervix is.'

'Well I do, in general terms. Just not exactly.'

Ruby frowns some more and removes the diaphragm, then she shows me exactly which bit is the cervix.

'This little bit in here that sticks out.'

Ruby tells me it moves around. I am fascinated.

'Does it move around fast? I mean, do you have to wait till it stays still for a minute, then try and get the diaphragm over it quickly?'

Apparently it doesn't. I try again and this time I am successful.

'Thank you,' says Ruby, standing up and adjusting her dress.

The room is covered in spermicide. Any sperm that comes in will have no chance of survival whatsoever.

I tell Ruby that I like her new sunglasses and remind her that my band is looking for a new drummer, just in case she comes across one on her travels. She leaves to visit Domino.

Cynthia, pursued by detectives, meets her true love

After a few days sleeping rough Cynthia meets some punks who live with some hippies in a huge old vicarage near King's Cross. She makes friends and moves in with them.

One night the hippies annoy her by banging drums when she is trying to sleep. Cynthia stares out of the window. A full moon stares back at her. She goes and eats the hippies.

My my, she thinks. That was a good meal. Something between brown rice and a lentil casserole.

Werewolf detectives surround the house. They are armed with machine-guns loaded with deadly silver bullets.

Cynthia is forced to flee. Tumbling down the stairs she meets Paris, a young newcomer to the commune. She falls in love with him on sight.

But she only has time to brush her lips against his before the detectives pound down the stairs after her, and she flies off into the night.

~

Sometimes I work for an industrial agency that gets me casual work in factories.

Ruby phones them up for me because I am not very coherent on the phone. When she does this she tells them she is my wife.

I get a job cleaning in a huge industrial garage in Gunnersbury. The floor is black with oil and I have to clean it till it is white. It takes me around a day to clean a space the size of a car, grinding away at years of grease and filth with a scrubbing brush and a mop and a bucket. Also I have to clean the toilets.

The first day I make the mistake of cleaning the toilets too early and at the end of the shift all the workers come in and make everything dirty again. So after that I leave cleaning the toilets till last.

The company tells the agency that I am a good worker and the man in the agency is pleased and says that it is very rare for one of their clients to pay a compliment to one of their workers.

At lunchtime I sit on my own in the canteen and listen

to everyone talking about what they saw on television the night before.

One day a white worker calls out, 'Hey, Mandela!' to a black worker and there is a big argument because the black worker says he is not called Mandela, he has a name of his own.

I do not mind this cleaning work as everybody just leaves me alone to get on with it because I am obviously a good cleaner, but after about a month I don't go in one day because I wake up with the sure knowledge that Cis will call round and visit me.

'Not working today?' asks Ruby.

'No. Cis is going to visit.'

I spend the day thinking what I will say to Cis when she calls and rushing to the window at the slightest sound outside. I make up all sorts of speeches in my head, but eventually I decide that I will just tell her how pleased I am to see her again.

Ruby appears at around two in the morning with wet feet and sunglasses.

'She didn't call?'

I shake my head.

'Don't worry,' says Ruby. 'She might call tomorrow.'

I don't feel like cleaning any more floors or toilets so I don't go back to the garage and afterwards I have trouble even remembering where Gunnersbury is, although I miss the meals in the canteen because they had good pies and I used to enjoy sitting there eating them.

★

41

Marilyn and Izzy live in a housing co-op flat with three tiny rooms and red curtains. I wonder about visiting them. This is always a slight problem because I am friends with Izzy but I don't know Marilyn so well and if I visit and only Marilyn is in then I feel awkward. I decide to go anyway.

They are on the first floor with no bell so I have to throw stones at the window and I am careful not to throw anything too big because Marilyn gets really fucked off if she's watching TV and a big rock crashes into the window.

She gives me a friendly smile at the door. Upstairs Izzy smiles at me as well, and this is not so bad, two smiles in one day.

There is an advert for pensions lying on the floor. It shows a happy couple on a yacht, drinking wine.

I have no idea why people pay for pensions when you don't get the money back for more years than you can think about. I have no idea how people get enough money to buy yachts. I have no idea why yachts cost so much money. I have no idea why I spend even a second thinking about yachts.

'What are you thinking about?' says Marilyn.

'Pensions and yachts.'

'So you are still feeling bad about Cis leaving you?'

'Yes.'

Izzy has put up a poster in the hallway of a female body-builder. She is wearing a purple leotard that shows off most of her body. Her back is V-shaped, muscular and strong.

Marilyn and Izzy both play in a band and so do I so we talk about how difficult it is to get gigs and how appalling all other bands are and how much we detest all the other bands in the area.

'How is the weightlifting going?'

'Very well,' says Izzy. 'I am twice as strong as I was two months ago. I'm on a special healthy diet and I'm thinking of joining a club. Except I can't find a good club. There was a women-only bodybuilding class at the local institute but they closed it down. And I don't want to go somewhere where men will laugh at me.'

'They wouldn't laugh if you were serious about it.'

'Yes they would. Dean thinks it's hilarious.'

'How is Dean?'

'I haven't seen him for a week. Do you think I'm looking stronger?'

'Yes,' I lie.

'Say hello to Ruby for us,' they say, as I head off home.

Cynthia thinks about her love, and suffers at the hands of the weather

I love the boy whose lips I brushed, thinks Cynthia, lying alone on her rubbish tip. I have only seen him for three seconds, but my love is more powerful than any love that has ever been.

She writes him a love poem on the outside of her sleeve.

One time Cynthia ate a boyfriend because he brought her a love poem and it was really bad.

Feeling sentimental, she now regrets this.

I will never eat another human, she vows. Or rather, I'll never eat another nice human being. I may chew on a few nasty ones, but only if they really deserve it.

She wonders how she can get to see Paris. The werewolf detectives are bound to be watching the old vicarage.

Rain starts falling in large slow drops and the wind carries some of the moisture under the railway arch that overhangs the rubbish tip. Cynthia shivers and seeks refuge under some sheets of cardboard. She dislikes the rain, especially when she is living rough.

A few yards along from her more bodies shiver in their temporary cardboard shelters, tramps and derelicts who live with her on the rubbish tip under the arches.

In friendship they sometimes offer her some of their methylated spirits to warm her up, but Cynthia is not a big drinker.

∼

Back at my flat I ask Ruby if she thinks I should invest in a pension plan but she doesn't think it is a good idea at my stage of life, even though I specifically remember the advert said it was never too early to start. And I'm worried about forgetting to sign on because now we will have been thrown off the Social Security register. It will take weeks to get our claim sorted out and we will have no money for anything and we'll have to sit around for hours in the DHSS.

'Don't worry,' she says, 'I have a good idea for making money.'

'How come you got back with Domino?'

She shrugs.

Ruby tells me to read good books, although why she wants me to do this I am never quite clear.

She is always reading good books and she is a writer. She never shows me any of her writing except for the ongoing werewolf story, but I know she will be good.

Now she is busy plucking her eyebrows, so I give her artistic advice and make us some tea.

'How was the rehearsal?'

'It was good except we don't have a drummer anymore and I can't play my guitar so well now my soul is missing.'

'Maybe you left it in your guitar case.'

I hurry through to my room and look.

'No. It isn't there.'

'Well, don't worry, it is bound to turn up somewhere, probably when you least expect it.'

'I could ask the Goddess of Electric Guitar Players if she's seen it.'

Ruby frowns.

'There is no such thing as the Goddess of Electric Guitar Players.'

Later on Domino arrives and criticises Ruby's eyebrows even though they are looking terrific. After a while they start fucking in the living room so I can't go in and watch television, but the picture isn't very good anyway since Ruby battered it with a brick when she couldn't find a good programme.

I sit in my bedroom and play my guitar some more, trying to remember the new things I worked out with Nigel.

The Goddess of Electric Guitar Players is called Helena. She looks after you when you are trying to learn a new song and if anyone throws a bottle at you when you are going onstage she reaches out a graceful hand and diverts it onto an amplifier. Also, if you have been assiduous in paying tribute to her, she will prevent your guitar strings from breaking and give you a gentle nudge if your solo is starting to bore everyone. She brings comfort to everyone whose fingers are sore from trying to learn a new chord and, if the occasion merits it, she will personally get inside your fuzzbox and make it scream and shriek.

A lovely goddess, Helena.

After a few minutes the people upstairs bang on the ceiling because I am disturbing them.

I sit and feel lonely. Sitting and feeling lonely is something I am a spectacular success at. I can do it for hours. Everyone is good at something.

There is a knock on the door. It is Izzy. I make her some tea and show her my cactus.

'Ruby says it is a sacred Aphrodite Cactus. Once it flowers Cis will fall in love with me. It is a wonderful coincidence that she picked it as a present for me.'

Izzy says that love is not necessarily all that good a thing and asks if I can lend her two hundred pounds because she needs an abortion.

Through in the living room there is a furious argument with screaming and shouting and banging. The front door slams.

Ruby storms into my bedroom. Her face is streaked with anger and tears and she screams about what a bastard Domino is and how she had better not see him again or she will kill him, then she sits on the edge of my bed and complains that I don't have any comfy seats in my room. I wonder where Cis is. Cis had a comfy seat in her bedroom. But probably she is not in the comfy seat, probably she is in bed with someone nice, wrapped around him. Probably she is in bed with someone who is secure with a lucrative pension plan.

Izzy looks depressed and Ruby looks furious and I think about Cis and how difficult everything is but, lacking anything sensible to say, I keep quiet and let Ruby rage.

There is a tiny spot on the side of my cactus. It looks like it might be the start of a flower. There is nothing on Ruby's and I feel sorry for her, although really if Domino were to fall permanently in love with her it would be a very bad thing.

Cynthia hungrily thinks of home, but manages to find a meal in the end

Next morning Cynthia is dreadfully hungry. Remembering her promise not to eat reasonable humans, and not having any money at all, she wonders what to do about breakfast. She still has a few friends from her days at the vicarage, but she does not want to go begging food off them, though she would like to see Paris again.

She looks around for a stray cat or two, but nothing moves save for the homeless inhabitants of the railway arches folding up their cardboard beds and storing them carefully for the following night.

Back home on the croft her mother fed her regular meals. Today is Thursday. Every Thursday her mother made lamb stew and baked a cake. Cynthia craves for some lamb stew and a piece of homemade cake.

Three young men walk past and one of them wolf-whistles at her. Cynthia can see immediately that they are not very pleasant. She decides that it will be all right to eat them, and probably every bit as good as her mother's lamb stew.

So she does. Afterwards she vomits for three days till the lining of her stomach is dribbling through her nose.

~

My next contact is with a man who describes himself as fortyish and looking for a younger lover. He doesn't show. Probably this is just as well as I do not feel like a younger lover. I feel like a washed-out old person.

I feel bad when I wake up, so on the way to the toilet I kick the door and I almost break my foot and this is such a ludicrous thing to do that it cheers me up.

I limp through to Ruby's room with some tea. Ruby is in bed with a robot made out of metal boxes. Unprepared for this, I wonder if I should stay. I hover around for a few minutes, resolving finally to go out for a while and come back later with another cup of tea.

How did the robot get in? Usually I would hear anyone knocking on the door in the middle of the night. Of course, if it is a flying robot it could have come in the window.

I pour another cup of tea and look round at the mess in the kitchen. Neither me nor Ruby is very good at tidying up.

Back in Ruby's room the robot has gone and Ruby is talking to Izzy. Ruby holds the sheet over her, although I have seen her naked body many times. For some reason this must not be permissible when Izzy is in the room.

Izzy wants some breakfast, but Ruby refuses because she says she cannot bear to eat in the morning, or any other time really.

'How is your knee?' she says.

'What do you mean? There's nothing wrong with my knee.'

'I thought it was sore,' says Ruby, and drinks her tea.

I walk down to Brixton. My knee starts to hurt.

Marilyn is out buying apples and she asks me if I've seen Izzy but I say no.

I go to buy some apples.

Cis is serving behind the counter.

I am stunned by her beauty and memories of good times.

'Hello, Cis. Four apples please.'

I point to the kind of apples I want.

Cis puts four of them in a scale and weighs them, then puts them in a brown paper bag.

'How long have you been working here, Cis?' I ask, heart pounding.

'What are you talking about?' says the assistant who, on close observation, looks nothing at all like Cis.

'Nothing,' I mutter.

The assistant classifies me as a harmless crazy person and gives me a fairly sympathetic smile. I hurry away.

This cactus is sacred to Aphrodite because on one occasion she was pursued through the southern desert by Ares, God of War and unwanted suitor.

Unsuited to such a rigorous chase and unable to fight him off (Aphrodite is no coward, but Zeus refused to give her proper fighting skills, leading to her being pursued from the field of combat at Troy) Aphrodite falls to the ground.

A brave shepherdess, seeing her plight, rushes up, rips a nearby cactus out of the ground and rams it between Ares's legs. He is forced to retire from the scene, badly hurt.

'Thank you,' says Aphrodite. 'Why are you crying?'

'My lover left me by this cactus,' wails the shepherdess. 'It reminded me of him. I used to sit and watch it grow. Now it is dead.'

Aphrodite, graciously sympathetic, replants the cactus and it comes back to life.

'When it flowers your lover will return,' she says. 'And now and forever, in memory of my rescue, this cactus will be sacred to me, and will bring good fortune to all lovers who are gentle and kind.'

'We will make money from writing,' announces Ruby.

'What writing? Is your book ready?'

'No. Magazine writing.'

I wait for her to explain. Ruby is very smart and I know that her idea will be good.

'I have been down to the library and stolen all their magazines. And I have stolen some more from the news-agents. I got sex magazines, karate magazines, football magazines and romance magazines. And photo-love stories.'

'So? Are we going to sell them? It won't get us much money. Couldn't you steal something more valuable?'

'No. What I mean is, we will write stories for them and they'll pay us.'

I am dubious. But Ruby insists it will be easy, in fact what she has in mind is copying stories practically word for word and just changing a few names here and there and then sending them off.

'The stories are all crap,' she tells me, 'so there is no reason for them to reject ours.'

Cynthia falls ill, seeks help, and learns she is still pursued

Cynthia werewolf has only one friend in the world of werewolves, her kindly Uncle Bartholomew.

An eccentric professor, Uncle Bartholomew lives alone with his experiments. He never got over his wife leaving him for a movie star.

'Let me in, Uncle Bartholomew, I'm sick.'

'Cynthia, what are you doing here? It's not safe. Only the other day the detectives were here looking for you. Lupus the Werewolf King wants you dead.'

'I'll be dead soon enough, Uncle. I can't eat.'

Uncle Bartholomew makes her some tea and wraps her up in a warm blanket. He can see she is not well. This makes him sad. He always liked Cynthia and her rebellious ways.

'Tell me your problems.'

'I can't eat. I vowed only to eat bad people but they make me vomit. For some reason the only people that taste nice are my friends. Now I don't have any friends left. I'm so lonely I could die. And I'm in love, but I can't go and see him because I know I'll eat him. Help me before I eat all the nice people in London, and die of loneliness.'

Uncle Bartholomew offers her some vegetables but Cynthia has never been keen on vegetables. Anything green makes her want to scream.

~

My foot still hurts from kicking the door, in fact it hurts worse than before. My knee seems to be better. Ruby's idea about writing stories seems quite good to me.

It is March. My cactus shows no sign of flowering. The spot on the side has disappeared. Ruby's is barren as well. Perhaps they only flower in the summer. Although if they come from a desert in the southern hemisphere this might be their summer. I don't know if this matters. Do the months change round for a cactus when it is transported to another hemisphere?

Months later we are still flying through space.

The Captain comes to see me.

'Why are you not doing any scientific experiments?' he demands.

'I am busy writing a new song.'

'You are meant to be doing experiments.'

'I'm bored with them. Anyway, when we reach a new planet it will probably be full of primitives. They will not care at all that we have discovered new scientific data. But if I play them a few songs it is bound to get us off to a good start.'

The Captain leaves in disgust. I can tell he hates me.

When my fingers are sore from playing the guitar I ask the computer to give me something to read. It puts a file on the screen called ancient myths.

Ascanazl, I read. *The ancient Inca Spirit Friend of Lonely*

People. He would appear to anyone who was lonely and talk to them.

That would be nice.

Another crew member comes into my cabin and I play her my new song. She says she likes it because the guitar notes remind her of rain on Earth, and she misses the rain. She forgives me for almost getting us all killed in the meteor storm.

She even asks me if I would like to come through to her cabin and lift some weights together, but I decline the offer. I have no enthusiasm for exercise.

And I am very sad, because I left my girlfriend back on Earth and I know I will never see her again.

I call up the book of myths and legends on the computer screen again. *Ascanazl's mother,* it says, *was well known for her friendly manners. She lived quietly at the end of the rainbow, but every so often she would go round villages bringing food and medicine to poor peasants.*

On one occasion she was bathing naked in the woods when a mortal hunter came across her by chance.

'It is forbidden for mortals to see the unclothed form of a goddess,' she said. 'But never mind. Just go on your way and we'll forget all about it.'

Ruby sends me out to steal some more magazines. On the way to the shop I pass the flower stall and I stare at the daffodils for a while.

A large jet flies overhead and I stare at it as well, but I am surprised and perturbed to see five small fighters fly over and start attacking it with rockets and lines of tracer fire.

The airliner does its best to fight off the unexpected attack but as its only armament is a small machine-gun that the navigator pokes out the door it has little chance. Soon a rocket blows its tail off and it hurtles to the ground. More pieces break off before it hits, scattering the area with burning debris that starts fires in all the houses.

Luckily the paper shop is unaffected and I quickly pocket a few magazines while the assistant is still stunned by the explosion following the crash.

At Ruby's suggestion I am wearing my army trousers with big pockets specially for the occasion.

Loaded down with dubious magazines, I hurry home.

Cynthia feels sad about Paris and learns about her psychic appetite

Cynthia watches television in her Uncle's house. The daytime soap operas are full of difficult romances. This reminds her of Paris, and makes her immensely sad.

She wonders if he is in sleeping with anyone. The thought of Paris fucking someone else makes Cynthia want to plunge a knife into her stomach and twist it round and round. And maybe jump off a cliff as well and take poison and jump under a tube train and slash her wrists with broken glass.

Uncle Bartholomew shambles through in his carpet slippers.

'I've analysed your blood sample,' he says. 'And I know what is wrong with you. You've eaten too many hippies. Your system is infused with LSD. LSD has a very bad effect on us werewolves. You've developed a psychic appetite.'

'What is that?'

'It means you can sense who is a good person and who is not. And only the good ones will taste nice to you. In fact, the nicer someone is, the better they'll taste.'

Cynthia is about to enquire further when the werewolf detectives arrive. She is forced to flee, silver machine-gun bullets bouncing and ricocheting around her.

'There may be other symptoms,' calls out her Uncle after her.

～

After the young girl's body was found outside my Battersea squat the police asked me some questions. Not very many questions, really. A few days later I saw four men in a car in the street who looked like policemen. That was all.

I got a temporary job helping in a chemical factory somewhere near Chiswick, and carried drums of chemicals around and mixed them in huge metal vats. The person who worked with me was a fifty-year-old Kenyan who read Latin at tea break and classical Greek at lunch. He had studied for a law degree but switched halfway through to mathematics. Then he had some personal problems and was unable to finish his degree. Now he just read Latin and Greek in his breaks at the chemical factory.

The third member of the shift was heavily tattooed with

blood-dripping roses crawling down his arms and he told me he never went out with his wife anymore because she had put on too much weight.

Every morning, because of the times of the trains I could catch to work, I was three minutes late arriving and for this I would be docked fifteen minutes' pay. But as the alternative was arriving twenty-seven minutes early this seemed like the best thing to do.

The foreman thought I was a good worker and encouraged me to take the job permanently, but after a few weeks some chemicals splashed out of a drum and burned my eyes.

My burning eyes were the most painful thing I have ever experienced, by a long way.

There was no doctor in the factory and nothing in the medical supply box but bandages, so I went to the toilet and washed and washed them with water, hoping that I would not lose my sight. Then I went home on the bus with my eyes burning under a bandage, lifted at one corner to let me see, and lay around crying and burning for a while.

I gave up the job. The Social Security suspended my benefit for leaving work without good grounds.

My eyes got better. My next job was the one laying cement, which was horrible as well. I didn't get my eyes burned but it ruined my boots. After every shift I would shake with exertion and if it rained on the way home my feet would ooze with mud and cement.

★

All the buildings in the street are burning after the fight in the sky, but I make it home safely through the police and fire engines and ambulances screaming this way and that.

Back home Ruby is in her bedroom, listening to music.

'There were some aeroplanes fighting in the sky,' I tell her. 'But I managed to get some magazines.'

Ruby goes and puts the kettle on. She says that she is hungry and wishes we had some food.

She gets her typewriter out and we start copying some stories.

I read out some stories and Ruby types them out, changing them a little. It takes longer than we think it will and after making up a karate story and a doctor–nurse romance I am bored with the whole thing because as far as I can see the stories we are copying already say everything there is to say about karate tournaments and doctor–nurse romances. But Ruby wants to do some more because she is convinced we can earn money and Ruby and me both need money. Sometimes I have jobs but Ruby never works. I think she is becoming more and more disinclined to leave the house. Everything we need, I bring in.

Ruby hunts out another magazine from our bundle. It is called *Blow* and is composed entirely of photographs of men spanking women or hitting them with canes.

'One of Danny's,' she says. 'We are bound to get published in it.'

Danny, the person whose door I ripped off in frustration

some years ago in Battersea, is now a sex magazine editor. We still know him.

'But it is total nonsense,' I protest. 'And objectionable in every way.'

'No one will ever know. And these specialist sex magazines are sure to pay well.'

I read out the story and Ruby puts it down, changing it round a little.

There is a knock on the door. When I answer it I find Cis outside, delivering our new telephone directory.

'Cis has just brought us a new telephone directory, Ruby.'

'Stop being foolish and get on with the story,' demands Ruby.

I have no idea why she says this. It is true, I have the telephone directory as proof.

When we have a break for a cup of tea we go and look at the cactuses.

No flowers, and it is the beginning of April. Ruby, however, is getting on well with Domino and does not seem too worried. She sympathises with me.

'It will flower soon. Probably Cis knew that it was a sacred Aphrodite Cactus and gave it to you deliberately.'

Ruby tells me that we have to move next week.

'Why?'

'Pauline is coming back.'

It is Pauline's flat. We are only living there temporarily. I forgot all about it. We can never find anywhere proper to live.

'What will we do?'

'I'll find us somewhere,' says Ruby, matter-of-factly.

In the Battersea Squatters' Association we planned to defend a house against Wandsworth Council after they gave the tenant notice of eviction. The Squatters' Association was determined to resist this eviction because everywhere there were homeless people and everywhere there were empty houses.

We formed a defence committee and appointed one person in charge of the physical defence and one person in charge of publicity and made ready to resist the eviction. 'I met Izzy today,' continues Ruby. 'She was buying some new weights. Well, actually she was standing on a corner about to burst into tears because she's pregnant and Dean doesn't want to see her anymore because he has a new girlfriend. But after that she was going to buy some new weights.'

'Was she looking any more muscly?'

'No. Izzy is one of the least muscly people I've ever seen. But it keeps her happy.'

We have a break from writing.

'Relationships are terrible,' I say, and Ruby agrees. I ask her if she thinks it would be a good idea for me to go and visit Cis but she says probably it wouldn't be.

'How about if I phoned?'

'That might be better.'

'Will you phone for me?'

'What good will that do?'

'I don't know. But I'm terrible on the phone.'

'I bought some new earrings when I was out,' says Ruby. 'Look, little rainbows. One for you and one for me.'

Cynthia eats a motorbike messenger

Cynthia is in worse trouble than ever. She can only eat people she likes.

The rest of the werewolves scattered throughout Britain hardly ever eat people at all. They live as normal humans. Unfortunately Cynthia has never been able to adapt.

A motorbike messenger stops to ask her directions. New on the job, he has lost his way between Marble Arch and Brixton. He has a nice smile and a friendly manner.

Cynthia eats him while his radio crackles in the background.

A pleasing snack, she thinks, riding off on his motorbike. That's strange, I never knew how to ride a motorbike before.

Suddenly she realises that she never meant to eat him in the first place.

She would rather have made friends and seen more of his friendly smile. Her appetite has become completely uncontrollable.

~

Outside it is raining with maybe a few hailstones and I wish the sun would shine so I could see a rainbow because I like rainbows and if I don't see Cis soon I will go totally mad.

'I wish I could see Domino,' says Ruby. 'And I'm fed up with all this rain. This must be the wettest year in history. I'm going to go and paint some sunshine.'

I make her some tea and she strides through to her room to paint. I am envious of Ruby's ability to paint. I am envious of all artists. I have a good plan for seeing Cis.

Lamia the Eastern Huntress Goddess used to exercise daily to keep her body perfect. She fell in love with a mortal painter and asked him to paint her. Unfortunately, none of the paintings could capture her perfect beauty. Eventually, dispirited by his failure, he took his own life by drowning himself under a waterfall. Afterwards Lamia cried for her lover for forty days and forty nights and her tears fell like rain, washing away crops and houses in a flood of grief.

Izzy told me she heard that Cis was going to art school. I hope she does well. I would hate it if Cis became discouraged and drowned herself under a waterfall.

'Ruby, I have a good plan for seeing Cis and also it will probably help you to see Domino, and my zip is stuck, can you help me with it please?'

Ruby kneels down in front of me and tries to loosen my zip. Her room smells of paint and I notice she is losing weight.

The person in charge of the physical defence of the squat in Battersea went slightly overboard and barricaded the bay windows with railway sleepers, filling up the gaps with cement and barbed wire. To fit the railway sleepers in he organised the removal of half the floorboards and part of the ceiling. With the windows barred and barricaded and the doors nailed shut the house was practically invulnerable. The only way in was by ladder into the upstairs window.

We made a yellow banner with 'Battersea Squatters' Association' written on it. On the day of the eviction we would hang it out of the window.

Three people were nominated to stay inside the house when the bailiffs arrived. The rest of the squatters were to stand outside protesting. Nominated as one of the three, I was less than enthusiastic. I knew that when the bailiffs couldn't get in they would call the police and we would be arrested. But I had not done much for the Squatters' Association and it was my turn to be useful.

Ruby has to struggle with my zip for a long time but I trust her implicitly to fix it without doing me any damage. And if by chance she did do me some harm then she would call an ambulance right away. She is the sort of person who would have no problem in calling an ambulance and demanding they came right away, no excuses accepted.

Ruby is a wonderful friend and I worry about her losing weight. Ruby is the best friend I've ever had. Ruby is the best friend in the history of the world. It enrages me that she will lose weight and maybe harm herself all because of Domino. I hate Domino.

'There, your zip is free. If Domino saw me in such close proximity to anyone else's penis he would go crazy. Do you like my sunshine painting?'

'Yes, it's wonderful. The lilac sun matches your dress. How is your writing coming along?'

'Fine. I'll show you a story soon. When's your gig?'

'We had to postpone it again. We still can't find a drummer. Do you want to hear my plan for seeing Cis?'

'OK. What's your plan for seeing Cis?'

'Well, first you ring up and check if she's home. If she answers the phone you put it down immediately like it is a wrong number, but if she's out then there's a good chance we could accidentally run into her. It is Thursday and Cis will cash her Giro today and probably go for a drink. There are four pubs in Brixton she might go to and we can call in to each one casually as if we were just there for a drink ourselves and if she is there I'll naturally just have to say hello. She won't realise I've planned it. If she isn't at any of the pubs she might be at some friend's house so we can call round her friends on some pretext, and if that fails we could wait at the end of her street and see if she happens by.'

'What pretext are we going to use for calling round on her friends?'

'I don't know,' I admit. 'I hoped you could think of one.'

'And what will you do if you meet her?'

'I'll say hello.'

'What then?'

'I don't know. I haven't planned that far ahead. But there is a good chance we'll run into Domino along the way.'

'Fine,' says Ruby. 'It seems like a good plan to me. Let's do it.'

Cynthia does not accomplish very much

Cynthia werewolf rides around on her motorbike. She loves to take corners dangerously and threaten pedestrians. Unfortunately she cannot stop thinking about Paris. She is tormented by the thought of him sleeping with other women. When she—

~

There is a sudden silence as Ruby comes to a halt.

'What's the matter?'

'I have writer's block. I don't know what happens after Cynthia rides away on her motorbike.'

'Make her eat a few more people,' I suggest. 'I like it when she eats people.'

Ruby frowns, and plays with the material of her dress, and she tells me she is feeling bad. She is troubled because Domino has not been around for a few days. He might be sleeping with someone else. Just like Cynthia.

'Do you think about Cis fucking someone else?'

'About twenty or thirty times a day.'

'What do you do to stop thinking about it?'

'I don't do anything. Nothing works. I can remember every inch of Cis's body perfectly. I can picture her fucking someone else like it was happening right next to me. Usually after a while I get to wondering if it hurts very much when you slit your wrists.'

'It would here,' says Ruby. 'We don't have any sharp knives. We'd better get drunk instead.'

We hunt out our money. I like whiskey but Ruby likes brandy, so I buy a bottle of brandy at the off-licence. The off-licence is full of Irish women buying Irish whiskey. They have all come over to have abortions in Britain because it is illegal in Ireland. In London they are lonely, separated from their friends and families, forced to travel abroad like fugitives. They buy the Irish whiskey to cheer them up.

I wish them good luck and take home a bottle of brandy. Then Ruby and I drink it as fast as we can till it makes us fall asleep. It is quite a good idea of Ruby's, because you can't really think of anything when you are collapsed drunk on the floor, and next morning you have a terrible hangover, and this is good for taking your mind off other things as well.

Come the day of the eviction the publicity person had done his job fairly well and other squatters from south London were there to help us picket. Some pressmen from small local papers arrived with cameras.

All the squatters were cheerful but I was nervous. The week before one of the women in our group had been arrested for causing a fight at the dole office, and she described to me how the police put her in a cell all night and the cell seemed as big as a matchbox. I did not want to be locked up all night in a tiny cell.

Upstairs in the barricaded house we three occupants had a pile of things to throw at the bailiffs. Plastic bags full of paint and piles of rotted fruit and, strangely, cold porridge.

I became more and more nervous and wondered if I could escape over the rooftops when the police arrived. I wondered if it would be normal police or the Special Patrol Group, because the Special Patrol Group was very active in south London at this time.

Sitting in the window I looked up at the sky and wondered if some beings in a spaceship might fly down and rescue me.

'I like your new earrings,' says Marilyn, who has called round for a visit and a cup of tea.

'Thank you,' I say.

'Thank you,' says Ruby.

'Your flat is cold.'

'We're having problems with our bills. How is Izzy?'

'Stuffing herself with steak to help her muscles grow. And depressed about Dean, and her pregnancy.'

Ruby and Marilyn disappear and Cis is there in their

place. She is wearing a lilac T-shirt I gave her with a cloud on the back and a rainbow on the front.

'I have wandered in here by mistake,' she says. 'I was on my way to spend my Giro at the pub.'

'Right,' I say. 'Perhaps I'll run into you there.'

'Nothing would induce me to eat a steak,' says Ruby. 'I hate steaks.'

Three bailiffs in suits arrived and shouted at us to come out.

'We have nowhere to live!'

They did not seem inclined to discuss it. But before we could throw anything at them they went away. Inside the house we were shivering with cold.

Some hours later still nothing had happened and the pickets from other areas began to drift away. By midafternoon it seemed certain that the bailiffs must have abandoned their efforts for the day and would not be coming back till the next day. We were tired, having been awake all night, so all three of us left to get some sleep while another member of the group climbed the ladder to keep look-out, just in case.

I was very relieved not to have been arrested by the Special Patrol Group, although I knew that after a break of a few hours I would have to go back.

But I didn't have to go back. Half an hour after we left to go round the corner to our squats, the bailiffs returned with some police and the look-out immediately fled out over the roof and down into the back alley. The bailiffs repossessed the house without any difficulty.

As an act of resistance it was a pathetic failure. And it ended the Squatters' Association because while previously we had been negotiating with the council for possible rehousing, the council was now extremely irate at all the damage we had caused to the house in fortifying it.

'What about our rehousing negotiations?'

'Pay us twenty thousand pounds for the damage you did to the house and we'll think about it.'

We were all evicted soon after and no one made much fuss. The local news programme showed pictures of the inside of the house, all cemented and barbed wired and no longer habitable. This is what these vandals do when they squat, they said.

This all sticks in my mind very clearly. I'm not sure why.

I moved to Brixton with Ruby and we still could never manage to find a secure place to live.

Cis had a nice council flat in her own name. I liked sleeping there. But she argued too much with her sister and moved back in with her mother. I don't know what the arguments were about. I suppose there was lots of Cis's life I didn't know anything about.

Maybe it sticks in my mind because it was all so futile. But it wasn't a ridiculous effort. There shouldn't be empty houses when people have nowhere to live.

Possibly removing the floor and the ceiling was a tactical error.

Cynthia looks for a leather jacket and eats another lover

'I suffer from terrible claustrophobia,' says Marion, a very agreeable young woman who sells clothes in Kensington Market.

Cynthia has gone there looking for a cheap leather jacket.

The jackets are all too expensive but she is pleased to meet Marion.

They eat carrot cake and arrange a date.

Out at a disco they have a happy time together. Cynthia thinks that if she can't be with Paris, being with someone else she likes is bound to make her feel better. And she is determined not to eat Marion, no matter what happens.

'Would you like a snack?' says Marion, back at her flat.

'Yes please,' says Cynthia, and eats her without thinking.

She goes back to her rubbish tip to cry. Her psychic appetite seems to have left her with no control whatsoever. It only needs someone she likes to offer her food and she will eat them.

Why oh why was I born with such terrible problems, she thinks. And where oh where is Paris, the great love of my life?

Some council workers arrive to clear away the rubbish. Cynthia is forced to move on. A homeless refugee and the unhappiest of werewolves, she skulks around in alleyways, rummaging for food in dustbins.

Afterwards she notices that she has started to suffer from claustrophobia.

~

I wonder about Izzy's pregnancy.

'If we sell enough stories we can lend Izzy the money for an abortion,' says Ruby, telepathically.

'Maybe she will build huge muscles and win a body-building competition.'

'I doubt it,' says Ruby. 'Not in the next month, anyway.'

I am helping her with her hair. She has a mass of matted dreadlocks and ties thin colourful ribbons into it. I like helping with it.

'I will post the stories,' says Ruby, 'because I don't trust you not to lose them.'

She takes the bundle in a large brown envelope and I wander out to see what I can find.

Down in Brixton market I meet Rosaline from the Dead City Dykes and she tells me to come to their gig next week and I say I will although every day someone tells me to come to their gig; the place is full of people putting on small gigs for their bands and telling me to come to them.

'I just wrote a new song,' she tells me. 'It's called "My Spaceship is Full of Plastic Daffodils."'

Next I meet an actress called Kath I know slightly. She tells me she is going to be in a play and I should come and see it because it will be a good play. It is about gypsies having problems living their life and always being moved on because no one wants them living next door.

I used to be an acting student, that's how I met Cis, we were acting students together. Our class was being taught by a famous director from Poland and Cis and I were playing the parts of lovers.

After having a drink in the pub with Kath I find myself being tattooed. I am shocked at this because I never really wanted a tattoo. It hurts. The needle looks like a dentist's drill and where it pierces the ink into my flesh the skin bleeds. Blood and ink run down my arm over the muscle and onto the hand of the tattooist, a fat man covered in tattoos who grips my arm tightly so the skin doesn't move.

Behind him is his assistant, a young skinhead only half-covered in tattoos but catching up fast. His jeans are ripped to show off a tattoo over his knee. Today my knee has been hurting a lot.

'What your studio needs is a nice bunch of flowers,' I say, trying to make conversation. They are not great talkers.

Outside it is raining hard and two gypsies offer to sell me some sprigs of heather.

Back home I am very annoyed.

'Ruby, this has got to stop. I keep having these terrible hallucinations. I just imagined I was being tattooed, it was dreadful.'

'What are you talking about?'

She pulls up my sleeve.

'Nice tattoo.'

I look at it. It is a nice tattoo, under the matted blood. The blood is dark red going brown, just like the base of my cactus, which is dark underneath the green on top.

I apologise to Ruby.

'Did you post the stories?'

'No. I left them on the bus.'

'What?'

She left them on the bus. Somewhere in London bus drivers are sitting at their tea break poring over sex and karate stories with our address at the bottom.

'Unless of course someone else picks them up on the bus.'

We look out the window to see if there is an angry group of feminists preparing to storm the flat, outraged at our not-very-liberating sex stories.

The coast seems to be clear. We decide to go out for a while, just in case.

'I brought you a sprig of heather.'

'Thank you,' says Ruby. 'It is a nice sprig of heather. It matches my dress. I met a drummer yesterday who is looking for a band. I gave him our phone number.'

I show everyone my new tattoo and they all seem to like it.

The director from Poland told us we had to start living our parts more fully and made Cis and me become lovers right then, so we made love onstage in rehearsal with the other students watching and learning their lines. When we were acting in a bodybuilding play we lifted weights all day together.

Cynthia goes home to visit her mother, who gives her a useful present

Cynthia's problems increase. Not only can she only eat nice people, but she is starting to take on their attributes as well. After devouring Marion she is claustrophobic for a month.

Still, she is pleased to know how to ride a motorbike.

Where oh where is Paris, she thinks, staring up at the moon. I will die if I don't see him. On the other hand, if I do, he might well die. My appetite seems to be beyond my control. What is to be done?

Risking an attack of claustrophobia, she jumps on a train and goes to see her mother on the croft in Scotland.

'Mother, you have to help me. How can I have a love affair without it turning into a tragedy?'

Her mother is not pleased to see her.

'What sort of shade of purple is that for a werewolf to dye her hair?' she demands. 'And how often have I told you, you have to wear shoes? You're not in the forest now, you know.'

'Right,' says Cynthia. 'I can see you don't want me here. I'll leave.'

Moved by some remnants of parental affection, Cynthia's mother fetches a necklace from her jewellery box.

'Take this. It is the family's hereditary werewolf soul jewel. Give it to the one you love and you will never want to eat

them. Now, get out of here before I phone Lupus. You disgust me.'

Cynthia leaves.

'No real daughter of mine would put seven earrings through each ear,' her mother shouts after her.

~

When I wake up the cactus is in full bloom. Its flowers, yellow, lilac and mostly beautiful, exceed everything I have dreamed of.

Cis shouts my name through the letterbox and I run down the hallway to open the door.

There is no one there. I have imagined it all.

'Why are you wandering naked in the hall?' asks Ruby, her lilac dress crumpled from sleeping in it.

'No reason.'

'Make me some tea.'

I put on a pot of water. We have an electric kettle but we are having trouble paying our last electricity bill.

The God of Foolish People Who Walk Around Naked in the Hallway Thinking Their Lover Is Shouting Through the Letterbox is called Alexander and really there is nothing good to say about him at all. He is more of a demon than a god.

His brother is called Philip the Terrible and he is responsible for delaying people's Giro cheques in the post and sending out electricity bills that no one can afford.

Yesterday Ruby and I spent four hours wandering

Brixton trying to accidentally bump into our lovers but my plan was a failure. We met neither Cis nor Domino, despite calling into every place we could think of where they might be.

'Sometimes it's difficult to manufacture coincidences,' says Ruby, sharing a drink with me before closing time. 'A pity. I would have liked to fuck Domino right this minute.'

'We could try again tomorrow.'

'It won't do any good,' says Ruby, morosely. 'Nothing does any good. You fall in love with someone and they leave you and you feel like dying. You meet their friends in the street and you tell them how unhappy you are and you hope this news will get back to your ex-lover and they'll take pity on you. Or else you meet their friends in the street and you tell them you're having a great time and you hope this news will get back to your ex-lover and make them jealous. You think about things you could have done and what you would do differently if you had the chance, you wait for the phone or the doorbell to ring, you hang around the fringe of conversations hoping to hear some snippet of information about how they are.

'You can write poems and send them or not send them, you can turn up drunk at their house and plead with them to come back or turn up drunk and pretend you don't give a damn, you can send flowers or love notes or a few intellectual books, you can discuss it endlessly with your friends till they're sick of the sight of you, you can think about it all day and all night, imagining that somehow your mental power will win them back, you can sit on your own and cry or go out and make yourself frantically busy. You can think about killing yourself and warmly imagine how sorry they'll be after you do it, you can think about going on a trip round the world and probably when you got back you'd still hope to run into them on the street. You can do anything at all and none of it is any good. It is completely pointless. Lovers never come back. You can't influence them to do it and you would realise this if only you weren't so dementedly unhappy all the time.'

The pub is noisy with little room to move, and we have to guard our drink against a marauding barman who keeps trying to snatch it off the table even though there is a good half inch left at the bottom.

'So we won't try again tomorrow?'

'We might as well. What else is there to do?'

'Write poems?'

'What was it like in bed with Cis?'

'I can't remember.'

'That's a pity. If you could remember it it might cheer you up.'

The rain beats on my bedroom window and seeps through the warps in the frame to make small puddles on the window-sill. With my finger I draw the puddles into little shapes like spaceships and pretend they are flying free through the sky.

The drummer that Ruby gave my phone number to has joined the band and we are already planning to play our much-delayed gig. I am writing a new song. It is about Cis. It will be wonderful. We will make a record out of it and it will be a success. Cis will hear it, realise she really does love me and come back. I think this sort of thing all the time.

It will be a rush to get the song written and rehearsed in time for the gig, but it will be worth it.

I shout to Ruby to come and listen and I play her the chords. She says she likes it.

'Do you think it might touch Cis's heart and make her want to see me again?'

'It might.'

'If I don't see her again I'm going to commit suicide.'

'How?'

'I'm not sure. I thought I might carve my goodbye note on my chest with a kitchen knife, then go and die on her doorstep.'

'Well at least she'd remember you. But don't do it yet, I'll miss you.'

'OK, I'll leave it awhile.'

Nigel appears with a bundle of posters, drawn by us and photocopied at the cheap place in Coldharbour Lane. Tonight we will go and stick them up all over Brixton. I do not enjoy flyposting but I like seeing our name on walls. Also, if we don't do it no one will know about the gig.

Ruby says she will cook a meal so I can eat when I get

back, but when I arrive home she claims that just looking at food made her feel sick so she had to throw it all down the toilet.

'I spent the evening writing a story instead. It's about you and Cis fucking. You want to hear it?'

'Of course.'

'Right. Sit down comfortably.'

The lonely old lady on her balcony never looks as if she is sitting down comfortably. Maybe when you are old you can't get comfortable if you are lonely, no matter how many well-made chairs you have saved up for your retirement.

'It's my period,' said Cis, one day. 'I love having sex when it's my period. Let's fuck till we're swimming in blood.'

So we do. Cis is wearing a tampon. I take it out for her and it is red with menstrual blood. Cis likes her menstrual blood. So do I. In the air it quickly dries and goes brown.

I lick the blood from around the lips of her vagina. Cis likes this but the pressure of my tongue is often not quite enough to make her come so when she is excited I press harder on her clitoris with my finger and I slide another finger up her anus and then she comes quite quickly in a noisy flurry of blood and urine and some other liquid that I can't put a name to.

Next she sucks my penis. I like her doing this and when I come she keeps the sperm in her mouth and stretches up to kiss me quickly so she can spit some of it back into my mouth while it is still warm.

After a little while we start fucking. First Cis lies on top of me, then I lie on top of her. She puts her legs around my neck and while she is doing this she rubs her clitoris with her fingers till she reaches orgasm. She turns over so I can fuck her from behind. Her vagina is very wet and when I glance down I see that my penis and the inside of her thighs are covered in her blood. After I come she sits up and sperm and blood and vaginal fluid dribble from between her legs and we stick our fingers in the liquid and paint it on each other's bodies. I paint it round her nipples and she paints it round mine so when we next embrace both of our chests are smeared with a sort of brownish glue.

We fall asleep for a while and when we wake Cis wants to lie on top of me while I suck her breasts and reach my hands between her legs. She trembles slightly when I do this and digs her nails into my skin. I can smell the stink of our sweat-covered bodies and it is the thickest smell of sex I have ever experienced. As Cis comes I again slide my finger up her anus. 'Fuck me there,' she says. Needing lubrication, I smear more of her menstrual blood onto me and mix it with saliva and she rubs some cream on my penis so that it slides easily into her. I fuck her like this from behind and then she turns over, telling me that we can fuck anally from in front as well, which we do, while she stretches her arm around me and inserts her finger in my anus and pushes it in and out fairly violently, and slightly painfully.

After I come Cis wants me to lick her cunt again. Good. It takes around an hour for her to orgasm and she makes enough noise to wake the whole street. We fall asleep for a long time.

Next morning our bodies are smeared with every human excretion. On our thighs and genitals, and on the sheets, is a hardening mixture of blood, sweat, semen, saliva, vaginal fluid, penis lubricant, shit, urine and the bright red lipstick Cis bought in the market last week.

We wash our bodies but the sheet seems beyond help, so after a few days we throw it out.

Fucking with Cis is wonderful fun.

'Did you like it?' asks Ruby.

'I certainly did. It sounded terrific. No wonder I miss her.'

Our toilet is blocked because of all the food Ruby has emptied down it.

We discover that neither of us has ever cleaned a toilet. We are not keen to start now. Ruby suggests pouring bottles of bleach into the bowl and it so happens that we have lots of spare bleach because I had to buy six bottles to get a free booklet on looking after house plants.

After a day or so the toilet is clear again and Ruby promises to throw our food only in the bin in future.

Lovers never return. Stories about people who go out and win back their lovers are all lies.

Cynthia successfully makes love, and feels less lonely

Back in London Cynthia wastes no time in trying out the necklace. She disguises herself as a postman in case the were-wolf detectives are still watching the old vicarage, and sneaks in to see Paris.

He is delighted to see her.

Cynthia gives him the necklace. They fuck happily all night.

He is not a very good lover but Cynthia shows him how to be a better one. All werewolves are wonderful lovers.

When he falls asleep, late on into the morning, Cynthia lies contentedly beside him. Lonely no more, she thinks, and it is a very happy thought.

~

Ruby and I move house.

We grind through the process of sorting out our benefit claims, visiting the Unemployment Office and the Social Security Office. Sitting waiting to be called I worry that some clerk has already shouted out my name and I've missed my appointment, even though I know that I haven't.

Looking round vacantly at all the noisy and quiet

people sitting there, I wonder what it is that they all do. I am eager to get home in case my potted plant has flowered.

Our spaceship crashes on a sparsely populated world killing all the crew except me and the robot.

Outside the world is made up of bleak and empty plains split up by a few canyons where small groups of humanoids cluster amongst black vegetation, eking out their existence under a feeble blue sun.

The spaceship is beyond repair. I take the robot and go to the nearest community, looking for help.

At the edge of the canyon I am stopped by a force field. Scientifically primitive, the inhabitants have developed powerful mental abilities.

'Go away,' says an elder.

'Where?' I say.

'Anywhere but here.'

I trudge on across the plain. The robot is able to synthesise a little food from the rubble but, insufficiently powered by the blue sun, the food it provides is thin and unsatisfying.

On the edge of the next canyon the same thing happens. The inhabitants will not let me in.

I walk on alone.

'Make a radio,' I instruct the robot. 'So I can talk to Earth.'

The robot shakes its head. It cannot make a radio. It can't talk either.

It is not much of a robot.

The house that we move to is a flat on the Loughborough Estate and it is the only squat that I ever actually open myself. I borrow a jemmy and jemmy the door, ripping off the security cage the council has fixed over the door. With the jemmy it is easy and gives me a feeling of power. Ruby has obtained some fuses from a friend and she fits them into the fusebox.

'A brief prayer,' she says, lowering her head.

'Great and kind Tilka, Guardian Goddess of Squatters everywhere, please make our electricity work.'

Right away we have electricity. The whole thing has gone very smoothly, although being on the fourth floor and the lifts not working I have a lot of hard carrying to do.

Days later me and the robot reach the next community. There the elders also refuse me entry. They are dressed in yellow robes, with long silver earrings studded with opals.

'Please let me in. I have been walking for days and I'm coming down with fever.'

They refuse. Sweating with an alien disease, I sit down on the edge of the canyon and watch them going about their business, although under the poor light of the blue star I can't really make out what their business is.

When I rest against some of the black vegetation it crumbles into ash and settles quickly on the windless plain.

'OK robot,' I say, resigning myself to a friendless existence. 'It looks like I'll have to teach you to play chess.'

But it never really gets the hang of it and after a day or so I abandon the attempt and we just sit and watch the humanoids scuttling about, doing whatever it is they do.

The robot synthesises some medicine to cure my fever. It is not completely useless.

Around this time Ruby is involved in a fight with Domino and he hits her on the side of the ear and bruises her. When she arrives back in the flat she is trembling with fury and she has a cut on her foot from storming across the concrete outside. I am outraged but Ruby doesn't want to do anything about it, just not see him again. When any of her friends say that Domino deserves some violence himself, she brushes it off as an irrelevance.

She spends days writing in her room, and paints a little. Ruby is a good artist but generally doesn't bother doing anything when things are going well with Domino.

Because it seems like we might starve to death, I think maybe I should find a job. Ruby, busy writing, agrees to phone up the agency for me.

'How do thirteen-hour nightshifts in a private mailing

warehouse sound to you?' she calls, covering the mouth-piece of the phone.

'No, I don't want it.'

'Fine,' says Ruby down the phone. 'What's the address?'

Cynthia is happy living with Paris

Cynthia and Paris have a wonderful time. She lives in his room and he does all the shopping. This way the werewolf detectives will not find her.

Except when Paris is out shopping, they fuck all the time. Werewolves can have wonderful orgasms, and so can their lovers. And she never has any desire to eat him, apart from a few small bites here and there.

~

Later in the day Ruby helps me make some sandwiches. I am too gloomy about the prospect of a thirteen-hour nightshift to put much energy into sandwich-making.

'Don't worry, it's well paid and you only have to do it for a few weeks.'

'But thirteen hours? At night?'

'It's only four shifts a week. Anyway, it will take your mind off Cis.'

'I will not have enough time left to look after our cactuses.'

'Two cactuses are called cacti. And you'll have plenty of time left. I think your one is starting to grow a flower bud.'

Waiting for the bus to take me to my new job I am harassed by werewolves. They are not sure whether to eat me or not because they have already had a few good meals today but they think they might anyway.

Izzy appears in the distance.

'That's my friend Izzy,' I say to the werewolves. 'She is a champion weightlifter. She has immense muscles. If you give me any trouble she will beat you to death.'

The werewolves run away.

'Hi, where are you going?' says Izzy.

'I'm going to a new job doing nightshifts.'

'I'm going to the gym,' says Izzy. 'Look at my forearm development. Pretty good eh?'

'Yes.'

She is deluding herself. Her forearms just look the same to me. It is lucky the werewolves didn't look very closely.

Working at the mailing firm is like a punishment from God. The workplace is a draughty warehouse near Waterloo, and outside there is nothing but other warehouses with no one around so it seems that I am working alone in a desolate city, although only a few streets away there are busy shops and restaurants.

At the start of my shift I have to stand in a big wooden frame with pigeon holes everywhere. I collect a pallet of mail from round the corner, then sort it out into all the countries it has to go to.

It is all business mail. The businesses save money sending it through the mailing firm instead of the Post Office and the mailing firm makes a profit large enough for the owner to arrive in a Rolls-Royce, though I never understand exactly where this profit comes from.

Each job of sorting can take hours and the foreman is keen for the work to be done quickly because if it is not then he will suffer for it.

There is an hour for a meal and two fifteen-minute tea breaks, which makes eleven and a half hours' work.

At my meal break I think about Izzy. She doesn't want to have her baby. When I asked her if this was because she was getting on so badly with Dean she seemed slightly annoyed and said no, that had nothing to do with it, she just doesn't want a baby.

After many hours sorting it is time to load the truck. When the truck pulls up to the goods entrance and opens its back door it seems as big as a football stadium.

The mailbags are so heavy I can only just lift one to shoulder height, but loading the truck means carrying hundreds of them up a shaky ramp and then piling them up as far as I can reach above my head.

I am on 'E' shift. The other four workers are stronger than me. They sweat but they can cope. Towards the end of loading the truck I can hardly lift a mailbag above my knees.

Back home Ruby is writing a letter to her genitals and arranging the flowers I brought in to brighten up our new flat. Cis has forgotten all about me and is having fun with a string of devoted boyfriends.

It is four in the morning, my muscles are shaking and the forklift is bringing up another huge metal cage of sacks to be loaded.

'Mind your feet.'

The cage bangs down.

Here's a gentle ballad for all you lovers out there, croons the DJ from the radio on the wall. I pick up another sack and struggle into the truck, embarrassed that I am weaker than everyone else.

I feel ill. I want to phone up Cis and ask her to pick me up in her mother's car. If Cis did that all the other workers would be impressed by her beauty and would not mind so much that I am weaker than them.

She would take me home in her car. Then she would talk and talk like she liked to do, and we could cook some terrible food.

I can see her in front of me. Here, Cis, have some business mail.

Cynthia learns that life is still full of problems

Cynthia prowls happily around in the backyard. Paris is away buying tea bags and a new plectrum for her guitar.

She has not eaten a human for weeks. Contented with her life, she is prepared to make do with vegetables.

Everyone in the house is a vegetarian.

Paris is away for a very long time. When he arrives home

*Cynthia throws herself into his arms and kisses him passion-
ately, but Paris holds back slightly. She senses this immediately.
A werewolf can always sense when someone is holding back,
especially while kissing.*

'What's wrong?'

Paris says he has met someone else.

'Do you love her more than me?'

Paris isn't sure.

*There is a splintering crash. Cynthia thinks for a second that
it is her heart breaking, but it is in fact eighteen werewolf detectives flooding in through the windows.*

~

Ruby has many friends but she usually only sees them
when her and Domino are not speaking. When they are
together she mainly just sees him. I find this hard to understand because all of her friends are nicer than Domino.
Everyone else in the world is nicer than Domino.

I practise my new song but I can't get it right so I go and
make some tea for Ruby and she tells me about the contact article.

'But why a contact article?'

She looks at me patiently.

'I explained it all already. What's wrong with your
memory these days?'

I shrug. I don't know. It seems to have disappeared.

'You remember that guy who used to live next to you
in the Army Careers Office? The one whose door you

ripped to shreds the night you arrived home with Anastasia?'

'The one who used to overdose all the time and lie around shivering? Of course I remember him, I could never get a bowl of cornflakes in the morning without stumbling all over him. Isn't he dead by now?'

'No, he is the editor of *Triple X Adult Fantasy Magazine*. And he told me he would pay us good for articles about meeting lots of bizarre contact people and fucking them. Or not fucking them, depending on what they want.'

'What else would they want?'

'I'm not sure. Maybe they might want to piss on us and stuff like that.'

I look at Ruby.

'Do we really have to let strangers piss on us to earn some money?'

'Well, maybe not. I figure maybe we could make some of it up. But anyway, we'll answer some ads and post a few ourselves and see what kind of replies we get.'

'Can I put an advert in for Cis?'

'No.'

I think maybe I will anyway. She might be lonely. She might be desperate to start going out with me again but too shy to ask, frightened that I will not want anything to do with her.

'Go and steal some more magazines after you've helped me practise with my diaphragm. And see if you can find some nice flowers, these ones are dead.'

Walking round to the shops I can't find the flower stall but I do meet Helena, benevolent Goddess of Electric Guitarists. She is resplendent and beautiful in a ruby-coloured dress.

I pay her proper respect, then I ask her if she could maybe help me with the chord changes in my new song.

'I'll try,' she says. 'But I am finding it difficult to concentrate. My girlfriend has left me.'

'You too?'

'I'm afraid so. This morning she kicked down my door and told me she never wanted to see me again. Take these daffodils for your flatmate. I don't need them anymore.'

I buy a romantic fiction magazine and steal a sex magazine and take them back to Ruby. I feel sorry about Helena losing her girlfriend. Obviously it is a universal problem.

Ruby is pleased with the daffodils. I put most of them in the living room but I save two for my room, where I put them next to the cacti. 'Look at these nice flowers. Why don't you grow some nice flowers too?'

It is now May. Although it is pouring rain outside we are well into spring and I am sure it must be the flowering season for cacti.

'Look at that tree,' says Ruby, pointing out the window. 'It is covered with lilac buds. Just like my dress. What do you think it is like being a tree?'

'I don't know. Peaceful, I suppose. But you would get wet all the time.'

Next day Ruby says she will take me for a day out. I ask her if I have to bring a bucket and spade but she says no, we're going to the British Museum.

At first I am not enthusiastic, but when we arrive I start to enjoy myself. Ruby holds my hand and we walk round roomfuls of exhibits: ancient Egyptian mummies, Greek armour, Persian carpets, all sorts of things. Groups of schoolchildren hurry about them from this glass case to that and serious tourists look at their guidebooks.

Some of the children point at Ruby's bare feet and she smiles at them before their teachers drag them off to look at more exhibits. The teachers are looking after large groups of children, but they do not seem to be harassed by it. I suppose they are specially trained.

After a while Ruby hunts out the information desk.

'Can we get a cup of tea anywhere?' she asks. 'And where is the armour that Hector stripped from the body of Patroclus at the siege of Troy?'

'The restaurant is at the far end of the ground floor,' the assistant tells us, pointing the way. 'And Patroclus's armour is in the room immediately above.'

'Thank you,' says Ruby.

We have to queue a long time for our tea but it comes in a good silver pot. Ruby tells me the story of Hector and Patroclus at the siege of Troy and right after we go to look at the armour. It is still stained with ancient blood.

Next we look at huge carved lions that used to guard the gates of Babylon and in the ancient Syrian jewellery section we spend a long time staring at the earrings and deciding which ones we like best and which ones we'd like to wear if we could take them away.

When the museum shuts we buy a drink in the pub along the road. Ruby is happy, though I expect she wishes Domino was here.

'Who is the guardian spirit of museums?'

Ruby doesn't know. 'But whoever it is is doing a good job.'

It was a good visit. If Cis was still talking to me I'd ask if she wanted to come here and if she did she would like it a lot. She'd like to be at the seaside too, with a bucket and spade.

'If I'm stuck for some conversation with these contact people I can tell them all about the museum,' I say to Ruby, being practical.

Cynthia fights ferociously to save her life and finds herself in the sewers with rats

Cynthia is involved in a terrible battle with the werewolf detectives. Despite being fairly small, she is in fact one of the strongest, most ferocious werewolves ever to walk the midnight streets.

While Paris and the rest of the inhabitants flee, Cynthia plunges into her assailants' midst where it is difficult for them to bring their silver-bullet-filled machine-guns to bear on her.

Jaws crunching with rage, Cynthia sends several of her attackers to the werewolf afterworld before finally her legs are riddled with bullets and she has only strength left to plunge out through a window. She escapes on a motorbike.

Round the first corner she realises she no longer knows how to ride a motorbike. The effects of eating the motorbike messenger have worn off. The motorbike skids under a bus and Cynthia's ribs cave in under the impact.

Fortunately she is very resilient. It takes more than bullet-riddled legs and broken ribs to stop a ferocious young werewolf, particularly one that grew up strong on a lonely croft with porridge for breakfast every morning.

While the detectives pour out of the warehouse, Cynthia stumbles down a manhole into the sewers and paddles her way to freedom.

Rats flood out of every opening in the sewers, attracted by the blood that pours from her wounds, but Cynthia savagely fights them off and carries on swimming, blinded by blood, crazed with passion, and fearfully claustrophobic in the underground maze.

~

Ruby has disappeared. I have not seen her for three days. She is not at Domino's. None of her friends have seen her. I am frantic with worry. I trudge from place to place and after the first place it starts to rain. My clothes are soaked through and no one knows where she is. Dead images of Ruby in a torn lilac dress dance in front of me.

I meet Cis carrying some parts of a drum-kit but she won't talk to me. I meet a man with a terrible birthmark down one side of his face and bad acne on the other side and he trembles and tells me that nothing I suffer is as bad as the staring and avoidance of staring that he endures every day. I meet a former flatmate of mine with a suitcase who is walking down to the Maudsley psychiatric hospital for a brief stay as an inpatient. I meet Gerry who plays bass guitar and doesn't like me because he thinks I tried to steal his girlfriend years ago. I denied it to everyone although it was true. I meet Mary who has had a baby and produces so much breast milk that she is on her way to the children's home with a spare bottle for the motherless babies alone in their cots. I meet all of the Dead City Dykes who claim to be the only lesbian speed metal band in the country and they tell me they will shake the nation when they find a new guitarist, but they haven't seen Cis and they haven't seen Ruby. I meet Izzy who is on her way to see a doctor to start abortion proceedings after calling into the sports shop for some heavier weights, and she hasn't seen Ruby either. I meet Alice who works in a travel agency, and Maggie who is being evicted, and Jane who is selling communist newspapers and Barry, who has nowhere to stay, but none of them know where Ruby is and I become wetter and wetter and colder and colder and I end up in the centre of London looking in alleyways and other than this I don't know what to do.

★

A few years ago I walked round the centre of London with nowhere to stay the night, not knowing what to do. It was raining heavily and my clothes were soaked through. I wanted to be somewhere warm. Just being somewhere warm would make me very happy. I meet a person at the edge of Soho who is friendly and we get talking and share a cigarette. His name is Phil and he is a drummer. He shows me a comic he is carrying and he says I can read it if I want. It is a tale about some spacemen lost after a meteor storm. I read it in a café he takes me to where we can sit all night.

The café is full of hopeless degenerates and I feel quite at home. One of them is called Spider because of the spider's-web tattoo across his neck. His long hair is filthy and even sitting in his seat he manages to give the impression of someone shambling about in an alleyway. As the night passes he starts to shake slightly and tap his foot to an imaginary rhythm.

I feel all right in the café, at least I have somewhere to sit for the night. On each table there is a vase with one yellowed plastic flower drooping over the edge and I find these quite pleasant.

Another person walks past and offers Spider a cup of tea and nods to me and I get bought a cup of tea as well. Pretty soon the tea buyer sits next to us.

He is about forty with a small tough face and thin hair tied in a little ponytail.

'Call me Jocko,' he says, 'although it's not my real name. No one in London knows my real name.'

He seems pleased that no one in London knows his real name and regales us with stories of his time as a security guard at the local amusement arcades.

'I used to carry a chopper. I found that better than a knife. I've had people come up and point shooters at my head.'

About three o'clock he invites me and Spider home. Spider tells me that normally Jocko would not give him house-room, so it seems that I am the attraction.

Jocko's door is bright green and battered. The original lock has been torn off and a new one has been fitted underneath with some metal panelling to strengthen it. Jocko has lots of pornography. A magazine called *Bits of Boys* sticks in my mind. When I was eight I wouldn't have known how to give a blow job. Jocko is pleased that he has a nice room to stay in close to Soho, and very cheap, and pleased that he is at home with violence.

I sleep with Spider, although Jocko says I am welcome to stay in his bed if I will be more comfortable there.

Probably I will be more comfortable with Spider. He is very dirty but I am not very clean myself.

'Will I toss you off before you go to sleep?' says Spider, trying to be friendly, but I decline his offer.

Next day Jocko tries to make me stay in the flat but I say I have to leave. Seeing his small axe lying next to the knives and forks on the sink, I am very polite about it and promise I'll come back.

★

I desperately want Ruby to come back.

The nightmare in the mailing firm continues. After two weeks of thirteen-hour nightshifts I have turned into a zombie. During the day I seem to have no time to sleep because I am busy trying to organise our gig, and rehearse my new song about Cis, and look for Ruby. I struggle up the ramp, loading the truck. The DJ is playing records.

'Get a fucking move on,' says Mark, the shift foreman, as I start to wilt.

Mark knows all about being a shift foreman. He told me he learned it quickly because he doesn't just want to be a shift foreman all his life. And when he worked cleaning cars he learnt everything about cleaning cars in one day as well.

I pound down the last sack and collapse onto the floor. It is three o'clock, time for a fifteen-minute break. By the third shift of the week all five of us are so exhausted that we curl up on empty sacks and sleep during these fifteen minutes, although sleeping for fifteen minutes only makes you feel worse when you have to get up for the next lorry.

I think about Cis. I have never felt so lonely and hope-less as when lying on these mailsacks.

I want to go and tell Ruby about it. Ruby has disap-peared.

'She's visiting her mother,' says Ascanazl, Spirit Friend of Lonely People, making a brief appearance. I know he is lying.

Here's a record for you, says the DJ. *It's from Cis, and the message is, come back, I love you.*

When I arrive back at the flat Ruby is home. I hug her and tell her how worried I was. She says she was visiting her mother and didn't I see the note she left in my room?

'No.'

'Or the one in the kitchen?'

'No.'

'Next time I'll spray-paint a message on the wall.'

She tells me it was a pleasant visit except her mother moaned about her not wearing any shoes.

She has brought back some fishfingers as a present from her mother so we cook them into sandwiches.

The sacred Aphrodite Cactus was first brought to Britain by Brutus. Britain is in fact named after Brutus. He was a refugee from Troy.

Aphrodite, sympathetic to the defeated Trojans but unable to help militarily, gave the refugees food and supplies for their journey, and a few cactuses to help them with their love affairs.

Geoffrey of Monmouth won his true love, the daughter of a local noble, in this way. As soon as the cactus he presented her with flowered, she fell powerfully in love with him.

Mine will not flower. Neither will Ruby's. It is almost June. June must be a good flowering time for cacti.

I ask Aphrodite if there is any problem but she is too busy to talk to me because there are broken hearts everywhere. She refers me to Jasmine, Divine Protectress of Broken Hearts. Jasmine says she will see what she can do but she is also very busy. The number of broken hearts there are is increasing all the time.

'I know,' says Ruby. 'And there is not much to do about a broken heart. But don't worry. I heard that Cis is missing you.'

I finish the fishfinger sandwiches and bring them through on our metal tray, green with a tobacco advert.

'I think it is a little banal,' says Ruby.

'You told me you were keen on fishfinger sandwiches,' I protest.

'Not the fishfinger sandwiches. I love fishfinger sandwiches, as long as there is plenty of mayonnaise. I think your story is banal.'

'What story?'

She looks a little impatient.

'The one you told me last week. About your spaceship crashing and you walking around on the planet with a robot.'

I have no idea what she is talking about. I never told her any story like that. I have never been in a spaceship that crashed onto another planet. But I go along with it while we're eating our sandwiches.

MARTIN MILLAR

'Why is it banal?'

'Because you stare at people doing things in canyons and don't know what they're doing and really that is a very obvious image and not original at all.'

I am hurt, despite having no idea what she is talking about. The amount of times I have helped Ruby with her hair, not to mention her sandwiches and putting in her diaphragm, she could be more polite than to call me banal.

She starts writing a letter.

'Is it to your genitals again?'

'No. This one is to my orgasmic response. I am really fucked off at my orgasmic response. Sometimes it is pathetic. I am going to give it a good telling off.'

'I want to write something too.'

'How's your orgasmic response?'

'All right I think. I haven't had much use for it recently. I don't think I could write it a very interesting letter.'

'How about writing a hippopotamus story instead?' says Ruby. 'That would be nice.'

Cynthia descends into hell, develops a liking for country music and eats some more friends

Cynthia drags her broken body out of the sewers and back to her rubbish tip. She lies on a cardboard box and bleeds.

This is the end, she thinks. Life is unbearable. I am pursued everywhere and my body is mangled beyond repair. But this is as nothing compared to the fact that Paris doesn't love me anymore. All I want is a friendly lover and a roof over my head. Is that too much to ask?

'Why are you bleeding all over my cardboard box?' demands a tramp. 'I have to sleep on that tonight.'

Cynthia loses consciousness. The tramp, a kindly soul, takes her to hospital where she almost dies. The doctors wonder how a young girl came to be riddled with silver bullets and have her ribs smashed to a pulp, but they battle to save her life.

Unconscious in hospital, Cynthia sinks into a terrible nightmare where she descends into the werewolf underworld. All around are the faces of the people she has killed and eaten.

'Die now,' they say. 'You deserve it.'

On the verge of being trapped there forever, the power of her love for Paris drags her back. She refuses to give up life while he is still in the world, and recovers.

She discharges herself from hospital and buys a bundle of sad country music tapes. All night long she lies on a rubbish tip howling at the moon and listening to Patsy Cline and Tammy Wynette, a terrible state for any creature to be in.

Hopelessly and helplessly alone, Cynthia visits the South London Women's Centre for some company. There she meets a few friendly women who invite her to join their plumbing company. Cynthia considers the offer but as she is on the point of agreeing the full moon shines through the window. By this time a fairly crazed werewolf, Cynthia is unable to resist, and eats them all up. She goes back to her rubbish tip in despair. She is tired after being hounded through the streets by irate friends of the mangled plumbers.

She changes back into human form and listens to some country music. Later that night she sneaks around the streets near to Paris's house, hoping she might accidentally run into him. Unfortunately, she is not successful, even though she checks all of his favourite pubs.

The young werewolf is in misery over Paris. Her only true love and he fell for someone else. Cynthia loves him to distraction. She gave him part of her soul.

~

We have no food and I am hungry.

'Why don't you go round the shops for some chocolate?' asks Ruby.

'I am scared of the werewolves. Yesterday they almost trapped me at the bus stop.'

'Right. You better just wait till daylight.'

Ruby is surrounded by bits of paper and magazines and seems pleased with herself.

'Maybe I could risk the shops anyway. Do you have any money?'

'No. But we'll be rich after our contact article rocks the nation. I've sorted out the ads to reply to. Here's your bundle.'

There are about fifteen, mostly from sex magazines, a few from other things with contact columns. I read them.

BEAUTIFUL THIRTY-FIVE-YEAR-OLD RED-HAIRED WOMAN SEEKS YOUNGER MAN, PREFERABLY ARTISTIC AND ATH-LETIC. MUST BE SEXUALLY SUBSERVIENT.

SINCERE GUY, FORTYISH, SEEKS YOUNG FRIEND FOR MUTUALLY SATISFYING FRIENDSHIP. INTERESTED IN DIS-CIPLINE.

OLDER GUY, GOT BOOKS, MAGS, VIDEOS, SEEKS SLIM YOUNG GUY FOR TRAINING. ACCOMMODATION NO PROBLEM.

MOTHERLY FEMALE, FORTY-THREE, INTERESTED IN FLOWERS, MYTHOLOGY AND DISCIPLINE, LOOKING FOR YOUNG MALE FRIEND IN NEED OF LOVE, AFFECTION AND CORRECTIVE TRAINING.

MUSCULAR GUY, INTO BODYBUILDING AND WALKS IN THE COUNTRY, SEEKS SINCERE YOUNG FRIEND TO EXPLORE THE WORLD OF SUBMISSION – PHYSICAL, MENTAL AND PSYCHOLOGICAL. ALL LETTERS ANSWERED.

'Do you notice anything about your ads?' asks Ruby.
'No.'
'Right. I'll help you write some replies. Go and get those photos you had taken last year when you weren't looking such a shambles as you are now.'

Still hungry, I go out to rehearse with Nigel. He tells me our drummer has left the band to go to acting school instead. We will have to postpone our gig again.

'I wanted to play my new song to Cis.'

Nigel has brought his drum-machine so we can rehearse on our own. It is a small drum-machine, an out-of-date model that cost him thirty pounds from the second-hand shop. All it does really is keep a beat. Compared to some drummers, however, this is not too bad.

We are rehearsing in a makeshift room downstairs in a squat that we rent for four hours at a time. The microphones will not stay on the stands so we have to tape them in place and sometimes the amplifiers stop working, but it is convenient and very cheap.

I get on well with Nigel. If we could find a drummer we would be a good band. No one would care if we were a good band and, playing the sort of gigs we would get, no one would ever hear us. But we would still be a good band.

Rehearsing is fun sometimes. Putting your guitar up full and thrashing it takes your mind off everything else and there is always the thought that today's rehearsals might be tomorrow's big success. And sitting round on rickety old chairs in a shabby rehearsal room smoking cigarettes between playing is fun as well.

Carrying my guitar home through Brixton is a little worrying. If someone stole it off me I could not afford another one. I like my guitar. It is a Burns, an unusual old British make. Actually it looks better than it sounds, but it has a nice aura.

Walking home I carry on a conversation with Cis in my head.

'It's cold tonight. Can you feel the drizzle? We can cut through this road here. It's quicker. Yes it is, really.'

I imagine her smiling, willing to go along with my shortcut although she doesn't really believe in it.

These imaginary conversations go on all the time.

I have the sudden inspiration of calling on Cis and telling her I'm locked out. She will be sympathetic about this and let me sleep on her couch, or rather her mother's couch, as that is where she is living just now. Her mother answers the door and refuses to let me in and tells me not to come back. I head on home and cut through the little park, past some trees.

Ruby is standing beside a tree. Her feet must be cold in the damp grass, unless they have become immune to all feeling.

'What are you doing, Ruby?'

'I'm seeing what it is like to be a tree.'

I stand beside her for a while. Nothing much happens.

'I think this is a little boring.'

'Yes,' agrees Ruby. 'I had hoped for better.'

'Should we go home? I'm hungry.'

'There isn't any food. But we can have some tea.'

We walk home, holding hands.

At the bottom of our tower block I think I see Cis but she is holding hands with Fanfaron, God of Electric Guitar Thieves, so we run up the stairs as fast as we can. The police would never be able to protect us from the God of Electric Guitar Thieves, and anyway there is never a policeman around when you need one.

Next day Cis phones me up and screams down the phone for a while and then she sends me a letter telling me how much she hates me. I am pleased to hear from her. I wonder if she would like me to send her some flowers.

Ruby is quite sympathetic when I tell her all about it. Domino is with her and they seem to be back together again and outside the next block the old woman is having a friendly conversation with Ascanazl, ancient Spirit Friend of Lonely People. She has made him a cup of tea and is telling him how hard it is to manage on her pension.

He tells her that she should have joined a private pension plan while there was still time.

I phone up the people we hire our PA off to tell them our gig is cancelled again and they are quite annoyed about it and say I have to send them some money anyway or they will sue me.

I wonder if they are serious. I do not want to be sued. I go to ask Ruby what to do but she is busy fucking Domino and I sense that she will not want to hear about my PA problems right now. Another important question springs into my mind however, so I go into her room where Domino is lying on top of her.

'Ruby, about this contact article, I have replied to all these gay adverts and I am not gay. Is this not a bad thing to do?'

'Well, you never fuck anybody these days so it doesn't really make much difference, does it?'

There is some logic in this.

'But they are bound to sense something is amiss.'

'Amiss? That's a funny word.' Ruby pushes Domino away and sits up, quite interested.

'I've never heard you say amiss before.'

'I must have picked it up somewhere. Perhaps Cis said it. Do you think Cis—'

'Will you get the fuck out of here!' screams Domino, who is probably wanting to get back to fucking, although as he doesn't live here and I do he has no right to shout at me. But I leave anyway and spend some time looking after Cis's cactus. I have a book called *How to Take Care of Your House Plants* that came free with six bottles of bleach and I am following its advice assiduously. If Cis was to walk in the door right this minute she would be proud of the way I have looked after her plant, although there is no sign of a flower.

Then I give some care and attention to Ruby's cactus, although she is at this moment fucking Domino there doesn't seem much need to help their relationship along.

I wonder if I killed her plant would Domino go away? I would like that. But I would not like to hurt Ruby.

I decide to make a sign.

I get some paper and write on it 'Cis's potted plant,' but I don't know where the apostrophe should go in Cis's because it is always a little confusing when the word ends with an s.

Back in Ruby's bedroom Domino has his head between Ruby's legs and she is looking like she is quite enjoying herself, but when I ask her where the apostrophe should go in the word Cis's she edges away from him a little to give the matter some consideration.

'C-I-S apostrophe S,' she spells out for me, hand on Domino's head. 'Anything else?'

'Do you know where the Sellotape is?'

'I think it's in the kitchen drawer.'

'Thank you. While I'm in the kitchen, do you want me to make you some tea?'

'Not this minute. In a little while.'

Domino has a terrible scowl on his face and seems to be shaking. I get back to making my sign. I do not really like Domino. I letter the sign with infinite care and Sellotape it onto the pot and I am very pleased with the result. When I give it some water and three carefully-measured drops of plant food I am sure I can hear it saying thank you.

'Grow me a little flower,' I say to it. 'I am fed up with not being able to eat and thinking that every person I see is Cis and being sad all the time. And it's all your fault.'

And then I have nothing to do. I rummage through some papers in my cupboard. I find a homemade ticket for one of our gigs, and a love poem. Ha Ha.

Cynthia, still sad, exhibits a social conscience and kills everyone in a wine bar

Cynthia calls in to visit her Uncle Bartholomew. He is having some trouble with his plumbing. Cynthia, fresh from eating some plumbers, knows all about pipes and drains, and fixes it.

'I've come to say goodbye,' she says, wiping her tools. 'My true love doesn't want me anymore. I'm either going to kill myself or become a pirate. I haven't made up my mind which.'

'Goodbye,' says her Uncle, unable to help her decide.

Down the road Cynthia develops a powerful hunger. She changes into wolf-form and sniffs around.

There on the pavement is a shabby tramp. He only has one foot.

I know I shouldn't eat humans, thinks Cynthia. But no one will miss him.

~

'Stop, Ruby,' I say. 'Don't make Cynthia eat the tramp with one foot. I get depressed just thinking about him.'

Ruby looks up from her story.

'Yes,' she reflects. 'So do I.'

We saw him last week in New Cross. He was lying on the pavement with an empty can of Special Brew cradled in his arms. His crutch was leaned up against a shop-front and his ankle stump stuck naked out of his filthy trousers.

'Another one slipped through the welfare safety net,' said Ruby, hunting in her bag for a little change.

'OK,' she says, looking back at her story. 'How about this? "Cynthia, moved by sympathy for the one-footed tramp, immediately bursts into an elegant wine bar just round the corner. She savages the rich customers to death

111

and steals their wallets. Stopping only to eat a spare plate of soup, she gives all the money to the tramp, and also a few bottles of wine." How's that?'

'Fine. I like it.'

'Right. But don't expect any more social conscience. Cynthia is crazed in love, and is not responsible for her actions.'

'Sit down comfortably,' says Ruby, opening her book of myths and fables, 'and I'll tell you a story.'

'Does it have a happy ending?'

'Yes.'

I sit down comfortably.

With all the standing around sorting mail and loading up trucks in the warehouse my knee starts to hurt continually and I begin to hate business magazines.

There is nothing interesting to read in the magazines, nothing interesting to look at in the warehouse, nothing to do but look forward to the next tea break or the end of the shift.

Where the truck comes in there is a metal door that opens by hydraulics, but at some time in the past a truck has run into it and ripped one side of it open so the warehouse is always cold.

One night a fox ran past the entrance and I found

something funny in a magazine. Even businessmen need cartoons.

I show it round but it turns out that three of the other four people on 'E' shift can't read. This is embarrassing and the embarrassment seems to be my fault. When there is a radio quiz on and I say some of the answers out loud I am generally mocked for being an intellectual. I am also mocked for my Scottish accent. In factories and building sites I am always mocked for my Scottish accent although it is usually friendly, people calling me Haggis and Hamish and saying 'Och aye the noo.'

'Abeline,' begins Ruby, 'a minor music deity who once used to play the harp to amuse Zeus on Mount Olympus, came to Earth looking for some adventure. He was bored after centuries of bliss on Mount Olympus and also annoyed because Zeus kept on doing terrible things to women he was attracted to, like pretending he was a swan and forcing them to have sex. Also he had a big argument with Apollo after telling him his harp playing was out of date.

'Abeline strolled around for thousands of years, playing music and having adventures until, some time in the late nineteen-seventies, he realised that there were no adventures to be had anymore and also music had become rather boring.

'Still unwilling to return to Olympus, he decided to

create an adventure of his own, so he gathered up four musicians and started up a band to make radical music. Abeline played mighty guitar chords that deeply impressed all who listened to them.

'Apollo came to visit Earth.

'"Abeline," he said. "I need you. An upstart young Tree Goddess from Vietnam has been telling everyone that her music is the most divinely beautiful in the Universe. She claims that it drove the Americans from her country. I disapprove of such presumption. We are going to have a contest and I want you to judge it."

'"I'm too busy with my band," protests Abeline. "And I'm not very interested in your sort of music anymore."'

Apollo tells Abeline that he'd better judge the contest if he knows what's good for him. Abeline, not wishing to bring divine punishment down on his head, is forced to agree.

'The contest is attended by all the world's major deities, except the Buddha, who is beyond competition, and Jasmine, who is too busy trying to comfort all the people with broken hearts.

'Apollo plays his divine music and the audience applauds rapturously. But when Daita, the Vietnamese Tree Goddess, sings there is no comparison. Her singing is the most beautiful sound ever heard in the Cosmos.

'"Well?" says Apollo, ominously.

'"Daita from Vietnam was the best," says Abeline, honestly.

'Apollo storms off in a fury but not before taking his revenge. He alters the sales figures so Abeline's band never make it into the charts and he maliciously influences the critics so they never receive any good reviews.

'What's more, Apollo curses Abeline so that no one will ever listen to his ideas about music ever again, so after a brief career as a music journalist Abeline fades into obscurity. And the enraged Apollo also inflicts all of Daita's descendants with a toxic fever so that, despite their best efforts, the trees will never grow in her country again.

'Daita, with no trees in her homeland, is unable to sing anymore, but wanders the planet giving help to the poor and oppressed, particularly labourers who have to work all day for low wages.'

Sitting round the table in the restroom with the other labourers on my shift, I listen to them talking about football and women and I try and join in, but I am not good at it and my contributions never ring true. When I make some comment about football there is usually a brief awkward silence, and if someone shows me a pinup in the paper I can never manage to say the right thing. One time Mark looks at a pinup and says, 'Imagine fucking that, be like throwing peas down the Blackwall Tunnel,' and everyone laughs but I am completely at a loss as to how to react and it must show because Dave says, 'What's the matter, you queer or something?'

I do not know why I can never join in the conversations between groups of men.

I tell my shift that my band has at last recruited a drummer but they are not really the sort of people who are interested in music.

It is the Sunday shift, our last. We finish all our work about two hours before the shift ends. I slump down exhausted on a pile of orange plastic sacks that scratch me through my clothes. A gang of robbers looks in briefly, but they leave almost immediately because we have nothing worth stealing.

The rest of the shift play with the mini forklift and shoot elastic bands at each other. Next week I don't go back because I can't stand it anymore so now I have the problem of signing on again. My knee hurts for weeks and I can't find a PA for the gig.

'Where is the happy ending?' I ask Ruby.

'I lied about it,' she says.

Cynthia becomes a highway robber, but suffers unfortunate consequences

Cynthia, lacking a ship, decides against becoming a pirate but does embark on a life of crime.

Hunted through the streets by the ever-vigilant werewolf detectives, she tries to forget her love for Paris by holding up cars and robbing the occupants.

She is wearing a purple shirt and green trousers. Ever since eating a man who designed book jackets, the young werewolf has been exhibiting terrible taste.

Reports of her crimes reach the ears of Lupus. The Werewolf King loses patience. He wants Cynthia brought to Justice. He instructs his detectives to bring her to him, or else.

Now these detectives are very wary of Cynthia. They have already lost several of their number to her ferocious fangs. They would rather just leave her alone. Lupus, however, is not to be defied, particularly when he is angry, so they formulate a plan.

Cynthia lies down on a lonely road. A car approaches, drawing to a halt at the sight of her apparently injured body.

'Stand and deliver,' she cries, leaping to her feet. 'Your money or your life.'

Cynthia can be quite theatrical when she wants.

Werewolf detectives pile out of the car. It is a trap. She is surrounded and captured, bound immediately in magical silver chains and thrown in the cellars of the Werewolf King to await trial.

~

Ruby's benefit claim is sorted out but mine is not. Ruby shares her money with me which gives us fourteen pounds a week each to live on, plus the six pounds I make as an artist's model. I scour the music papers for cheap PAs but all the cheap ones are booked up in advance and the only ones available cost eighty pounds. Eighty pounds is more than me and Nigel can afford. Perhaps John our new drummer can borrow it.

Nigel phones and says that John is leaving the band.

'He can't leave the band. He's only just joined. We have a gig in two weeks.'

'He's been offered a job drumming for someone else. He's going on tour.'

I tell Nigel about not having a PA either. Things look bleak for our gig.

Helena, Goddess of Electric Guitarists, is sympathetic and shows me how to play a difficult new chord but tells me again that she has no influence over drummers. And she is still sad because her girlfriend has left her. She has run off with Ezekial, God of Acoustic Guitarists, and I find this shocking because acoustic guitars are very boring.

'Who was that on the phone?' asks Ruby, who has a big yellow towel round her hair to dry it.

'Nigel.'

'Oh. I thought it might have been one of our contacts.'

'You sent off the postcards?'

'Yes.'

'Oh.'

When Ruby's hair is dry I help her tie the thin ribbons into it.

'What day is it?'

'I don't know.'

We look at the television to see what day it is but it won't tell us so I go round to the shops to buy a paper. The flower stall doesn't seem to be there anymore, perhaps without me to buy flowers for Cis it is no longer viable.

Cis is buying some sausages in the butcher's and I am wondering if I should have a word with her and maybe borrow a few sausages when I am suddenly kidnapped by four gangsters in a huge American car. I think it might be a Chevrolet but I do not really know much about cars.

'Is this a Chevrolet?' I ask, gun at my throat, but the gangsters are desperate men and don't reply, except one of them asks me briefly what part of Scotland I'm from as his parents came from Falkirk.

'Give us the rights to the new oil well or you'll never see your friends again,' says the leader, a small man of Italian extraction with an Uzi sub-machine-gun and a suit of violet that is brilliantly coloured although not as attractive as Ruby's dress.

'I don't have any rights to oil wells,' I protest. 'All I have is fourteen pounds a week and six pounds from the art class. Also, I don't have any friends.'

'You're lying. We'll cut your ear off and send it to your mother.'

The car is thundering down through Brixton. Too wide for the narrow streets we crash into the Ritzy Cinema, where this week they are showing a series of Marlon Brando films.

I am catapulted out just before the car explodes. Uzi machine-gun bullets hail in every direction as the survivors battle it out with riot police. Bystanders everywhere are mown down in puddles of blood.

I scramble for safety into the Ritzy.

'The film has already started,' says the woman in the kiosk.

'Damn. And I really wanted to see *The Wild One*.'

I decide to catch it later and shamble down into the market to see if anyone will buy me a pizza.

Izzy is there at the pizza stall. Although she has no money to buy me one, she tears me off a good chunk and I sit beside her and chew away at it. She tells me about a party tonight.

'I am feeling a little sad about Cis leaving me,' I tell her. 'How about you?'

'Dean is mad at me because I'm having an abortion.'

'I thought he had left you anyway?'

'He had. But he's decided it's his business if I have an abortion or not. Well he can go fuck himself.'

She pulls up her jacket a little way.

'Can you see an improvement in my trunk rotators?' she asks.

'Yes,' I say, although I do not know what a trunk rotator is. 'They are looking much better.'

'Marilyn borrowed me two hundred pounds off her parents to get me an abortion. Have you got everything ready for your gig?'

Immediately I am gloomy and can't finish my pizza fragments. Izzy reclaims them, saying she has to eat to develop muscles, although really it should be steaks and not pizzas. But she supposes every little helps.

Next to the pizza stall a few people hang around the door of a reggae shack and slightly shake to the music.

The robot and I trudge on across the blackened plain. I am fed up trudging. We have stopped communicating and the robot is entirely concerned with completing its life's work, a huge encyclopaedia of mythological mechanical deities.

Suddenly there is a total eclipse of the sun and the robot falls to its knees.

'Come on, make some light so we can keep trudging.'

There is a small whirring noise and a print-out appears from its side.

Silence, it says. *It is time for me to pray to the deity.*

It brings out a picture of Marlon Brando on a motorbike.

'You like Marlon Brando too?'

Who is Marlon Brando? it prints. *I am praying to the Harley-Davidson.*

The party Izzy told me about is in a squat in Kennington. The street, full of licensed squats, is buzzing with three parties, two black and one white.

At the kerb there are a few old cars and three majestic-looking motorbikes. Underneath the motorbikes a few shards of glass glisten in a small pool of oil.

Downstairs in the white party it is too full to move. There is a smoke-machine and beer on sale for a pound a can and one light shining horizontally across the ceiling. I stand around and talk for a while and I meet my friend James and his girlfriend Maz, who have a plastic bag full of drink which they share with me.

'Every time I meet Izzy she is always going on about her muscles,' says James. 'But they don't look any different to me.' I have a good conversation with Maz about caring for cacti.

It is bitterly cold on this planet. While the robot prays I shake and shiver and wonder how you go about building a new spacecraft. Suddenly I come across a small cactus, the only green thing I have seen on this world. It is small and beautiful and I stare at it for a long time.

Next morning I wake up in bed with Maz. This is a surprise. These days my life is full of surprises.

I hunt for my clothes, Maz gives me a nice smile.

'Don't worry about last night,' she says. 'It happens to everyone sometimes.'

'What,' I say. 'Having sex with your friends' girlfriends?'

'No. Getting drunk, being unable to have sex with your

friends' girlfriends because the drink has made you impotent, being sick over the bedclothes and screaming out that the cat is a demon out to drag you to hell.'

I have a terrible headache.

Walking home I see Cis right outside Brixton Town Hall doing an exotic dance with a bowl of fruit in front of a TV camera but I don't stop to watch because it is starting to rain and water is running into my eyes and making it hard to see.

Despite the rain the woman is still sitting lonely on her balcony so I wave to her and she waves back.

'What day is it?' says Ruby.

'I don't know. Should I go and get a paper?'

'No,' she says. 'Don't bother.'

Cynthia howls

Cynthia lies in the cellar, bound with unbreakable chains of iron and silver. In the morning she will stand trial. As Cynthia is too much of an embarrassment to werewolves in general to be let loose again, Lupus will most probably have her quietly killed.

Cynthia, however, is not concerned about this. She is not even thinking about it. She is thinking about Paris. She is picturing him in bed with someone else.

She lets out a mighty howl and rolls around in misery. Her heart feels like it has been pierced with a stake. Her soul is leaking out in a small silver stream.

The guards outside the door tell her to be quiet, but Cynthia ignores them and keeps on howling.

~

My first contact is called Steve. He is forty and interested in films. We meet in a wine bar in Camden and he takes me back to his flat where he tells me his theories about discipline. On Ruby's instructions I try and remember all the details and everything he says. He ties me onto his bed and whips me with a leather thong a friend brought him back as a present from Surinam, and then he puts a gag in my mouth and fucks me.

'Would you like to go and see a film next time?' he asks as I leave.

'Yes,' I reply. 'Is *The Wild One* showing anywhere locally?'

Ruby is fascinated by my tale of the night's events and goes so far as to leave the house to bring back some antiseptic cream from the chemist's. When she rubs it into my wounds she says she is surprised that such a violent person would advertise in a left-wing magazine like *City Limits*, but it just goes to show, you never can tell.

'Nigel phoned. He has found a good drummer and wants you to go and meet him tonight. Tomorrow I am going to see my first contact. Some man who wants to be dominated.'

I tell her about waking up in bed with Maz and also about how I had apparently drunk too much to be able to have sex.

'That happened to Domino last night,' says Ruby. 'Maybe we could form a club.'

Eventually me and the robot become bored hanging round the valley and we strike out boldly for the next continent.

On the whole planet there are no animals.

The robot converts into a boat and we sail across a dead sea.

The next continent is much the same, dead plains, small groups of shambling humanoids.

Unexpectedly, one village gives us a warm welcome.

'The great Rain-Singing God,' they say, and bring us some food.

I eat the food and sit around for a few days. Everyone treats me well. I seem to be some sort of star. They are friendly to the robot as well and I can tell it is happy.

After a few days, however, I notice they seem to be expecting something.

The headman approaches me respectfully with a bowl of fruit.

'Thank you.'

'When can we expect the rain?' he asks.

'What rain?'

'The rain to end our terrible drought. The rain that follows the Rain-Singing God.'

I admit frankly that I have no idea.

'But you are the Rain-Singing God?'

'No, I am a lost spaceman.'

He grabs the bowl of fruit off me and I am ejected from the village.

'You can't sing for rain,' I protest. 'Rain is the scientific result of certain meteorological conditions.'

Cis appears in a tattered spacesuit, singing happily. It starts to rain. Immediately she is bombarded with presents of fruit.

In her tattered spacesuit she looks immensely stylish.

I trudge away with the robot.

'Oh, fuck it,' it says, the only time I ever hear it speak.

The robot is becoming less and less inclined to synthesise food for me and I am becoming increasingly hungry.

Ruby has promised to cook me a meal because I have done all the cooking for the past month.

'What is that awful smell?'

'I have burned all the food you bought at Sainsbury's,' she says, 'and thrown it in the bin because it is all so unhealthy. From now on we are going to go on a Stone Age diet.'

'What does that mean?'

'It means we only eat the sort of healthy things our Stone Age ancestors would have eaten. Raw grains and fruit and stuff like that. That's what our bodies are made for.'

'OK, what healthy grains and fruits are we eating tonight?'

'None.'

'Why not?'

'We don't have any.'

'But I'm hungry.'

'Fasting is good for you.'

Right.

It is time to tend to our cacti. Now that it is July I am sure there should be some sign of a flower but there is not. Looking at my cactus, I start to feel some dislike for it. I suspect it is deliberately refusing to flower. It is unwilling to mend my rift with Cis.

'I am beginning to think this is all your fault,' I say, quite harshly. Ruby is watching television.

'I'm hungry,' she says.

I look in the fridge. I have never seen an emptier fridge. I think Ruby is only happy when all she has in the world is her dress and her sunglasses.

'You know, when I was being whipped with that leather thong I forgot all about Cis.'

'That's good. Something positive came out of the occasion. Also, I will be able to work it into a terrific magazine article. If Domino calls, tell him to go away. We had an argument and I never want to see him again.'

'What happened?'

'I took him some flowers and he spat on them. He threw my book of myths and fables down the stairs.'

She strokes her book protectively.

'He is upset because he drank too much to fuck. Did you know the Spirit of Evil Zoroastrism is called Ahriman?'

'No. But I'm pleased you told me.'

It seems that it is Clio, the Muse of History, who looks after museums. I tell her how much I enjoyed visiting the British Museum and I compliment her on her earrings, which are silver and gold with rubies and opals dancing at the ends. She tells me they are made by her brother Andryion who, as well as making jewelry, builds houses and always tries to help people who have no proper place to live. But often he is busy with his boyfriend Marsatz who is a painter. They are very happy together, always bringing each other little presents, but it sometimes means that housing does not get as much attention as it should.

Ruby hustles me out the house. It is time for the art class.

Today all the students have to do a series of fast drawings so that every few minutes the teacher shifts me into a different position. This is better than the normal two hours of motionless cramp. As some sort of prop the teacher puts a cactus next to me and she makes another little joke about hoping the cactus will not sting my naked skin.

Clio also looks after painters so she is interested in the art class. I tell her that all the exhibits in the British Museum were fine and also they serve good tea although it is quite expensive, and I confide that I am a little worried because I have heard that there is no money to keep museums open and they might have to introduce an admission charge.

'My friend Jane who sells communist newspapers tells me that the government hates giving money for things like art.'

Clio frowns.

'A strange accusation,' she says. 'I would have thought they were doing their best.'

'Well, she's not really my friend. I just run into her now and then.'

My feet are dirty. I hope no one at the class notices. I do not want them to talk about me afterwards and say to each other that I had dirty feet.

Back home with my six pounds I am very bored.

Ruby wanders through.

'I'm bored,' she says. 'Let's buy a new can-opener.'

'A new can-opener?' I say, a little surprised.

'Yes, I saw a brilliant new kind of can-opener on television, the advert had hundreds of them all dancing round doing the can-can. We have to get one, it will be wonderful.'

We spend a while getting properly dressed and wondering whether it will rain, then we hunt the shops for the radical new can-opener. I am dubious of course that it is really going to improve my life but I trust Ruby's judgement.

We find the new can-opener in Tesco. I am interested to be in Tesco. I have not been here since Cis and I were thrown out for shoplifting.

Seconds after slipping some bright yellow electric plugs and a packet of coleslaw into our pockets we were surrounded by security guards. We were surprised how quickly they came. We were also surprised to be merely thrown out and not arrested.

But I was not surprised to be caught. Tesco is full of bad demons and evil spirits.

It was no fun at the time but now it seems like quite a good memory. Except it reminds me of Cis.

Depressed by the memory of Cis I am unable to move.

'Come on,' says Ruby. 'I don't like it out here, I want to get home.'

'This new can-opener, please,' she says at the check-out. She does not want to steal it. I am relieved. Barefoot with sunglasses, Ruby is not inconspicuous.

'And twenty tins of beans and a loaf of bread.'

'Why did you get a loaf? Does the new can-opener slice bread as well? It must be a wonderful machine.'

Ruby says no, it doesn't slice bread, but as we are going to be opening lots of beans we can make toast and eat them. Sometimes I am lost in admiration for Ruby. I cannot think ahead like she can.

Walking home there is a man taking photographs in the street so we have to sneak past him because we do not want our souls to be stolen. Ruby has told me that when a stranger takes your picture the camera sucks up your soul and gives it to bad spirits like the ones in Tesco. I am anxious that this should not happen.

'Look at that boy's hair,' says Ruby. 'Isn't it nice?'

Tied up with plaits and white dreadlocks it is indeed very impressive.

'Get him to be your drummer.'

'But he might not play the drums.'

'Of course he does,' says Ruby, 'I can feel it in my feet.'

He says he will be pleased to audition.

Cynthia faces trial, and loses her guitar

Ruby tells me she is stuck. She is not sure how to rescue Cynthia from prison.

I think about it while I'm helping her with her hair.

'Can't you just have her eat all the guards in a savage fury and burst out through a window?'

'I was hoping for something more subtle.'

She ponders it for a while.

In the morning Cynthia is dragged upstairs to face the were-wolf court. Armed guards are everywhere.

Lupus is sitting on his jewelled throne.

'To my certain knowledge,' he says commandingly, 'you have eaten two hundred people. Despite my express desire that we

should not harm anyone in these civilised days, you have become the bloodiest werewolf in the history of our race. Have you anything to say for yourself?'

Cynthia is hard put to find a good answer. She has undeniably eaten a lot of people.

'I had a hard and loveless childhood in a lonely croft. As soon as I left I became tangled up in a series of tragic love affairs. I am not responsible for my actions.'

'Pathetic,' sneers Lupus. 'Is that the best you can do? Look at you. No shoes, purple hair, and fourteen cheap earrings. You are a disgrace.'

Cynthia is not pleased at this personal criticism. Her natural good taste has returned, and she has been taking a lot of trouble with her image.

Lupus picks up her guitar and brandishes it in her face. Whilst raging against her many crimes, he smashes it. Cynthia is appalled. She loves her guitar. Roused by an incredibly savage fury she attacks the guards. The room dissolves into a volcano of blood before Cynthia makes her escape by chewing through the bars and plunging out of a window.

~

'You were right,' says Ruby. 'A savage fury and an escape through the window was the best thing to do. Do we have any brandy left?'

'No. But I could get some. Is Cynthia still suffering the psychic appetite?'

Ruby shakes her head.

'No, I'm bored with that now. She can eat who she likes and it doesn't affect her.'

Halfway across another desolate plain we come across a ruined building. The robot forces in the door but there is nothing inside.

'Back on Earth I once had to force a door so I could get into bed with a young woman I met at a bus stop.'

I wait for some sign that the robot would like to hear the rest of the story but it does not give me one.

The robot does not think that I am a good storyteller. When I tried to interest it in a tale of some hippopotamuses it just looked at me with contempt.

Also it is busy compiling the encyclopaedia of machine myths and occasionally worshipping the Motorcycle God.

Everywhere on the planet it is raining. As a Rain God, Cis has been a spectacular success. I have given up hope of ever finding a home here and am resigned to trudging round for ever with a mad machine.

My only comforts are some ruby earrings that the robot synthesised for me to keep me quiet. Unfettered by any stylistic conventions I am wearing seven earrings in each ear. If there is room to pierce any more holes, I might put in some more.

I know that I will never have any fun again, and I wish that I was back on Earth.

★

Sure enough the new design can-opener is immense fun. It takes the whole tops off cans, and Ruby and I take it in turns to take the tops off and stare admiringly at the results because neither of us has ever had a good can-opener before, only the very cheapest one that you buy from a stall in a market and you have to wrestle with it for twenty minutes to open your beans and even then you still get your fingers ripped to shreds on the tin.

After all the tins are opened we pour all the beans into the sink and start on the other ends of the cans. By this time we are becoming hysterical and when there aren't any cans left we try it on the loaf and cover the room with crumbs and then we ask the people next door if they'd like any cans opened and when they say no, not right now, we ask them to be sure to bear us in mind when they do.

I have a few minutes' sadness when I think how much fun I could have had if Cis was here to see the new can-opener, but when Ruby gathers up all the tops from the cans and starts frisbeeing them down the hall I cheer up again and join in and all in all the new can-opener is probably the most fun I have had all year.

Afterwards, when the entire house is a slithering swamp of beans, breadcrumbs and mangled aluminium cans, I think that possibly life is not so appalling after all. Ruby gets me to massage her shoulders and she says I am easily among the best shoulder-massagers she has ever come across. I am pleased at this compliment.

I am not pleased to learn that she is back with Domino and he is coming round this evening to borrow a little money.

Out my window I can see the old woman on her balcony. She is looking lonely so I try and communicate with her telepathically, but she does not seem to be very adept at it and her replies are too weak for me to make out properly. I do get the strong impression, however, that her son is in prison for repeated chequebook fraud and that she disapproves of the Pope for being inconsiderate to the needs of women.

Cynthia finds that loneliness is good for your guitar technique

Without her guitar, Cynthia is unable to busk. Hopeful of remaining inconspicuous, she does not want to return to her life of crime. With Lupus still hot on her trail, really it would be best for her to leave town, but she cannot bear to be so far away from Paris.

There is only one thing to do. She finds a temporary job in a factory, making components for robots. Unfortunately, on her second day at the factory she is forced to chew the foreman's head off after he bores her for twenty minutes with a funny story about how he was thrown out of a nightclub at the weekend for starting a fight.

This brings Cynthia's industrial career to an end. She decides that she had better not work in any more factories because in her day and a half making robots she came close to eating almost everyone she met.

So she moves into a disused warehouse and lives on stray cats and dogs. She eats down the door of a music shop one night and steals another guitar, which she practises and practises on till she becomes a master of the instrument, and when the moon shines through the cracked windows above her head she exercises her voice by howling out sad country songs.

She thinks that maybe she will just stay in the warehouse for the rest of her life. Paris has no doubt forgotten all about her and she will never see him again.

~

My next job is as Assistant Head Storeman in a large hotel in Knightsbridge. There are two porters there who know the job already, but the hotel does not want to make either of them Assistant Head because they are both Indian.

I am embarrassed to be put in charge of them. I never once tell them to do anything.

'I think that story is worse than the last one,' says Ruby, who is dyeing a leather wristband.

'What story?'

'The one about Cis being a Rain God.'

'I don't have any story about her being a Rain God.'

'Yes you do.'

I don't have any story about Cis being a Rain God.

Ruby is getting crazier and crazier. It is probably Domino's fault, he is an awful boyfriend. I have known thousands of nice girls with terrible boyfriends.

Domino knocks on the door and when Ruby eagerly shows him her newly dyed wristband he says it is a mess.

'But wear it if you like.'

Ruby tries to hide her disappointment and quietly throws it away. It sinks down into the plastic bag full of yesterday's beans.

'We have a brilliant new can-opener,' I say, trying to cover the slight embarrassment caused by Domino's disregard for Ruby's endeavours.

Domino is not interested in any can-openers so I decide to go out and walk around. It starts to rain, which reminds me of Ruby's strange accusation that I have been telling Rain God stories.

At the next corner I meet Shamash the Sun God.

'I see Cis has been busy today making all this rain,' he says. 'I am lonely up there in the sky by myself. I could do with a friend. I am on my way to buy a book of mythical history that will tell me who the sun is meant to be friends with.'

'How will you get in touch?'

'I might place an advert. I think I would like to go out with a moon worshipper. Maybe even a werewolf. It's a long time since I had any excitement.'

'Hello.'

'Hello Izzy, what you doing?'

'I've just come back from having my abortion and now I'm going to eat a pizza in the market then I'm going home to exercise the muscles round my knees and thighs, what are you doing?'

I explain I have just been talking to Shamash the Sun God and Izzy says really, was it nice, and I shrug my shoulders because I don't want to make too much of it.

'Do you think if Cis was to walk along here with her little sister and her little sister was suddenly to run out into the road and then a massive truck was about to run her down because its brakes had failed and I rushed out and saved her then Cis would start going out with me again?'

'No,' replies Izzy. 'And anyway, Cis's little sister is seventeen and could dodge the truck herself.'

'Suppose she was drunk?'

'Is this likely to happen?'

'Well, yes, her little sister cannot hold her drink.'

'I mean, is the whole scenario likely to happen?'

'It was just a thought. I miss Cis terribly.'

Izzy says that she has noticed. When we reach the market she offers me some pizza but I don't enjoy it very much.

I do not last long as Assistant Head Storeman. The Head Chef, a very pompous man, is annoyed when he walks into the underground food store and catches me juggling oranges. I am reported to the Head Storeman. He gives me a terrible row and I resign in disgust. My benefit is suspended because the DHSS does not think that resigning in disgust is a reasonable thing to do.

'Ruby, why am I condemned to doing terrible jobs all the time?'

'Because the country is in the grip of evil demons.'

'Jane who sells communist newspapers blames the economy.'

'What would she know about anything?'

During my few weeks at the hotel I am, however, very well fed. Smoked salmon hang in the fridge and I eat strips off them and drink from gallon cartons of cream and devour boxes of expensive chocolates and every day I take a big peach home for Ruby.

When I get home after the pizza, I find that Ruby has moved house. This is a terrible shock. She has left without telling me.

But when I rack my brains I eventually remember that today was the day that we were due to move because our eviction notice arrived last week, in fact now I think about it I was meant to be out buying bin-liners to pack our clothes in.

The council have been and boarded up the door with a huge iron anti-squatting device.

Cynthia meets two international terrorists, and has to leave the warehouse

Cynthia's stay in the warehouse is interrupted by the return of Millie Molly Mandy and Betty Lou Marvel, international terrorists, drug smugglers and good-time girls. The warehouse is their secret hideout and they do not want to share it with a werewolf, even one they like.

I am doomed in everything, thinks Cynthia. Not only did my true love desert me but I will never even find a peaceful place to be sad.

'We're sorry about your tragic love affair but you can't live here,' says Millie Molly Mandy, dressed as always in a flowery frock. 'We need it as base for a new smuggling operation.'

'But I've nowhere else to go,' protests Cynthia.

She is considering eating them but they both have machine-guns and it is bound to be very messy.

'Here is some money,' says Betty Lou Marvel. 'Enough to live on for a while. We are going to assassinate someone now. Please be gone when we get back.'

There are many interesting stories about Betty Lou Marvel and Millie Molly Mandy and the trail of destruction they have left behind them, and all the fun they have had living it up on the proceeds, but they will have to be told another time.

They load up their sniper rifles and depart. Cynthia gathers together her guitar and spare sunglasses and leaves shortly after.

Outside she spends some time meditating in a Hare Krishna temple. They offer her some vegetables, but she refuses politely. Later she wanders round the British Museum, wondering what to do.

~

Ruby has gone and our flat is boarded up. I am alone in the world. I am engulfed in a huge flood of self-pity.

One of the many things I have in common with Ruby is that we are both expert self-pityists. We regard it as a good positive emotion. If I can't find her again I know I will never meet anyone as good for sitting round being miserable with.

Homeless, I stare at it, a little perplexed. I shake it but it won't let me in. Where has Ruby gone?

She is my only real friend. If she has gone away and left me I don't know what I will do.

I wonder if she took my belongings. I wonder if she took good care of my potted plant. I wonder if I was meant to help us move. It seems almost certain I would have been. Ruby will be furious. I have to spend five days sleeping on the floor of a slight acquaintance's flat and wearing the same clothes, and after I get rained on I am wet and shivering all the time.

Ascanazl appears, resplendent in his lilac-and-yellow feathered cloak. I ask him for help because now, without even Ruby to talk to, I am as lonely as I can possibly be.

'I'm afraid I am too busy to help,' he says. 'And my girlfriend has left me.'

My next contact refuses to fuck me because I am too dirty. Ruby will be furious.

'Please,' I say.

'No. You are too filthy for me to abuse. I have a horror of cold shivering bodies.'

Eventually I bump into Ruby in the street when she is out buying some margarine and she says where the hell have you been and why did you disappear when it was time for us to move? She seems quite annoyed about the whole thing and really I am stuck for a good explanation.

Eventually I have to claim that I was kidnapped by a spaceship and Ruby seems to accept this as a reasonable story.

She takes me to our new home, a squatted flat on the Aylesbury Estate. Having arrived five days before me Ruby has taken the best room, but I would have let her have it anyway. I notice she is looking a little fatigued. No doubt it was hard work moving all our things. Also she will have had to make all her own cups of tea and go round to the shops herself. Her dress is badly stained because she can never remember to buy soap powder.

I am a little sorry about all this so for the next week I try and make up for it by making continual cups of tea and helping her in every way possible. Soon she is feeling better and her dress is clean again. I buy her three new pairs of sunglasses and everything is fine.

We postpone our gig again. I rehearse with Nigel but we still don't have a drummer. The boy with attractive white dreadlocks turns up for the audition and he is quite good but he says he doesn't like our music and the weather turns colder and it rains everywhere and Cis's mother is living next door.

'Cis's mother is living next door,' I say to Ruby.

'No she isn't,' says Ruby, pulling down the top of her dress. 'Feel this lump, I think I have breast cancer.'

'Yes she is, I saw her.' I feel Ruby's breast but it doesn't seem like cancer to me, although I am not an expert.

'No you didn't,' says Ruby. 'You're imagining it. Do you think it is a malignant tumour?'

'No, I don't think so, but maybe if you're worried you should see a doctor. You're breasts are very white, you have skin the same colour as Cis's and I'm sure her mother is living next door.'

Ruby prods at the lump for a little while more and I can see she is worried, although she does take the time to tell me that the flats on either side of us are occupied by black families and as she seems to remember that Cis is white then it is not likely that any of the people there are her mother.

Reassured I go and look for a clinic of some sort and when I find one I ask for a booklet on how to check for breast cancer and the receptionist is very nice about it and loads me up with leaflets and pamphlets about all sorts of things. I am impressed by her efficiency.

'Would you like to be the drummer in my band?'

'No,' she replies. 'I am already a drummer in someone else's band and I wouldn't like to take on any more work because I am really involved in our music.'

'Oh well, thanks for the leaflets.'

'Be sure and have the young lady come in if she's still worried.'

'Right,' says Ruby. 'If I'm not going to die of breast cancer then we can get on with the insurance fraud.'

'What's that?'

'Come with me,' says Ruby. 'Mind the door when you leave, it's still weak after I jemmied it in.'

Ruby takes me round to the house of some friend of hers who I have never met and we immediately start loading up rucksacks with stereo equipment and videos.

The house is full of potted plants and flowers in vases.

'Will I take the flowers?' I ask, but Ruby says you cannot claim insurance for stolen flowers.

Cynthia meets Paris, is heartbroken, gets betrayed, but has a good meal at the end of it

Well, thinks Cynthia. I may as well go and visit Uncle Bartholomew. It is a long time since I have seen a friendly face.

On the way she bumps unexpectedly into Paris.

Cynthia throws her arms round him. They go for a drink together.

'Did you miss me?'

He says he missed her last week. This week, not so much.

Cynthia is more heartbroken than before and starts to cry in the pub. She is embarrassed at this, though Paris is reasonably kind about it.

Cynthia leaves and visits her Uncle.

He pretends to be pleased to see her but really he slinks off and telephones Lupus, because Lupus has threatened him that he'd better co-operate, or else.

So Cynthia is betrayed by her only friend.

When the detectives come, Cynthia, fired up after meeting Paris, eats them all without any trouble.

Fuck this, she thinks, finishing off her bad Uncle. I have enough problems without werewolf detectives chasing me all over the damn place. I am going to sort out King Lupus once and for all.

~

The pretended robbery continues until everything is packed into bags.

'Now we just wait for the van to take all the stuff down to Izzy's. Then we get a big cut of the fake insurance claim.'

The van doesn't arrive. After waiting for two hours Ruby says we had better just set off on foot. At one in the morning I have to walk the streets of Brixton with a rucksack full of stereo equipment and a video recorder in a black plastic bag, trying to protect them from the thick cold rain.

There seems to be a policeman on one corner and a gang on the next. At any moment I will be arrested or robbed.

Ruby strides confidently on, however, and we deliver the goods safely to Izzy's house.

'I'll help you carry them upstairs,' says Izzy. 'These days I'm pretty strong.'

'Now we have money,' says Ruby. 'And the rain has stopped. The pub round the corner is still open because there are bands playing. Let's get a drink.'

We overindulge in drink, relieved that we have not been arrested or robbed in the street.

The toilet in the pub has no glass in the window but still smells bad.

'Stop killing Irish children with plastic bullets' says some graffiti on the wall.

Two men in the pub make a comment about Ruby's bare feet and she tells them to go and fuck themselves. The band plays and they are quite good, which is a surprise.

'Do you know anyone with a chequebook and cheque card?' asks Ruby. 'I know where we can sell them for a good profit.'

'How is my cactus? It is August. It should have flowered.'

'Yes, it should. And so should mine. But they haven't. Perhaps something is holding them up. Did you notice Izzy had been crying?'

'No. What's wrong with her?'

'Dean hates her for having an abortion and so do her parents. She told me the whole world is against her. Would you like to hear a story I just wrote?'

'Yes.'

'Sit down comfortably, then.'

Cynthia flies a helicopter

Why oh why did Paris desert me, thinks Cynthia, landing her helicopter on top of Lupus's palace.

~

'Where did she get a helicopter?'

'She stole it,' says Ruby.

'How did she learn to fly it?'

She shrugs.

'Are you going to write any more about Millie Molly Mandy and Betty Lou Marvel?'

'No. They belong to another story. Now stop interrupting or I won't finish before dinner.'

'We don't have any food. You burned it all.'

'Good. Food disgusts me. Now listen.'

I wake up with Cis wrapped round me. A tiny bug walks over the quilt. I brush it off, taking care not to kill it.

When I sit up it wakes Cis.

'I have an idea for a new song.'

I get out of bed and drag my guitar out of its case, a good case, second-hand from the music shop in Coldharbour Lane, and start strumming. Cis joins me on the floor and works the tape recorder because it is fun to record a few chords and listen to them later.

Crawling around we are soon all wrapped up in guitar

leads and tape recorders and when Ruby comes into the room to see if she can borrow some money she laughs at us naked on the floor with musical instruments draped around us. Then we laugh too because it seems funny, although before we had just been having a good time and had not considered the fact that we hadn't got dressed.

My guitar lead stretches round Cis's thigh and between her legs, black against her very white skin. Beside her I look a grubby sort of light brown colour. Cis says that today she would like to buy some new earrings, small silver pendants with fake ruby stones she has seen in the market.

We play my new song, sit next to each other's bodies and think about making tea and buying earrings.

At four in the morning I walk past Cis's window. I stop and stare for a while, wondering what she is doing. Standing looking at her window is a ludicrous thing to do.

A policeman cycles up. I have never seen a policeman on a bicycle before. Bicycles are bad for the knees. After working in the private mailing warehouse my knee hurt for months.

'Ruby, do you know what I can do about my—'

'My knee is sore,' said Ruby. 'Can you go out and get me an elastic bandage?'

She had stolen my injury.

I walked round to the chemist but it was shut so I had to walk on further. At the next chemist I met Izzy.

'I'm just buying a bandage,' she told me. 'I hurt my knee doing exercises.'

It was an epidemic.

'What are you standing here for in the rain?' asks the policeman on the bicycle.

'Staring at my ex-girlfriend's window.'

He takes my name and date of birth and radios it in to the police station to see if I am a wanted criminal. I am not.

'You look bad,' he says. 'Try and get more exercise. Sleep with the window open. And good luck with your staring. I often stare at my ex-girlfriend's window myself. She left me for a guitar player.'

'Acoustic or electric?'

He doesn't know. He cycles off. It is still raining.

The stairs up to our flat make my knee hurt. My leg shakes inside as the muscles try to pull away from the cartilage.

Some time ago I bought Ruby an elastic bandage but I can't find it. I make straight for her bedroom, a room that, as is quite normal for Ruby's various bedrooms, has one wall painted black and the other three whatever colour they originally were, because Ruby's feeling that a black bedroom would be nice never extends beyond her first tin of paint.

I wake her up.

'Ruby, my knee is sore, remember you said I should see an osteopath, how do I find an osteopath?'

'Why do you want to know at five in the morning?'

'Because I'm feeling bad about Cis leaving me. I've just been staring at her window.'

'Never stare at someone's window in the middle of the night. It is a creepy thing to do. Also, you'll get arrested.'

'I almost was.'

Ruby struggles into her dress and brings a towel to dry my hair. Then I make us some tea and we talk about things and switch on the television.

An American comedy actress is being interviewed in front of an audience of fans.

'What is your inspiration for working?'

'The Big Guy in the sky.'

She says what a wonder and a privilege it is to be a mother, particularly in America. The audience applauds and Ruby says she is starting to feel sick.

I am a little hungry and offer to try and make breakfast, something I can do because yesterday we imposed some iron discipline on ourselves and went shopping.

Ruby declines the offer.

'The act of eating has started to repel me.'

'Has it? OK, I'll just get something myself.'

Ruby tells me I can't because she has burned all the food.

In the bin there is an unbelievable mess.

I was wondering what the bad smell was. It reminds me of the bad smell in the biology class where me and Cis first met, dissecting frogs.

She defied the teacher and refused to dissect a frog. She

said that dissecting frogs was a wicked thing to do. Naturally I went along with this and both of us refusing to dissect frogs in the face of strong opposition brought us together.

The local paper wrote a story about us, underneath a small article on flower arranging.

Ruby says that she would like some more sleep now, so I go and strum my guitar and walk around the room looking at the damp patches on the walls. The damp patches will be bad for my sore knee. I wish Ruby hadn't chosen last night to carry on her crusade against food. I feel better for talking to her.

Suddenly I have a good idea. I will look at Ruby's book.

If your sacred Aphrodite Cactus will not flower it may be being held back by the Archangel Gamrien. As a prime mover of patriarchal Judaic religion, he has little sympathy for Aphrodite, and none at all for sex.

Depressed, I put down Ruby's book of myths and fables. It is hopeless. I always wondered why everything went wrong all the time but now I realise it is because of all the powerful spirits ranged against me.

Before I go to bed I make sure the window is open.

Cynthia fights an epic battle

Cynthia silently eliminates all of Lupus's guards and creeps down to his bedroom.

There she finds him mournfully contemplating a photograph of his wife who left him.

She pads up to his shoulder and lets out a low growl. Lupus spins round. A moment's concern shows in his eyes but he composes himself regally.

'What are you doing here?'

'I've come for a little talk. Don't bother ringing for your guards. There aren't any left. You were right. I am the bloodiest werewolf in the history of our race.'

Lupus transforms into wolf-form, something he rarely does these days. As a wolf he is huge and malevolent. They fight.

They fight for three hours till the whole building is a tangle of blood- and fur-stained wreckage. They fight through every room and hallway till nothing is left whole and they fall to the ground, battered and exhausted.

Lupus is unable to move. Cynthia drags her body across to his. Slowly and painfully, she puts her jaws to his throat.

'Swear now to leave me alone in future,' she hisses. 'Or I'll kill you.'

Lupus knows when he is defeated. He doesn't want to die. So he whispers out a Royal Pardon. The Werewolf King will never break his word.

Cynthia grins, and starts to crawl away in triumph.

'Your mother died last week,' calls Lupus after her. 'She didn't leave you any farewell message.'

Cynthia leaves, her triumph spoiled by the death of her mother.

~

My next job is as a temporary clerk for Securicor in an office with a coffee machine on the wall and a sign in the bathroom: IF YOU ARE LONELY THEN GOD WILL HELP YOU.

Will he? Good. Please send me Cis.

I wait all day but she doesn't appear.

There are pages and pages of numbers in fractions. I have to convert them to decimals in the morning and file my results in the afternoon.

Every minute I am expecting bank robbers to arrive but they never do. I only stay there two days and later the agency tells me that I was not well enough dressed to work in the Securicor office.

Watching television with Ruby a man comes on and makes a joke about not being able to tell if the light in the fridge really goes out when you shut the door.

Ruby is outraged.

'What a boring tedious thing to say. I must have heard a hundred people say that.'

I am busy putting a patch on some jeans and do not pay much attention till some time later Ruby shouts at me from the kitchen.

'Come here a minute.'

She is staring at the fridge.

'I'll shut the door and you see if you can see a light through the crack.'

But when she shuts the door there doesn't seem to be any crack to see through. We spend about twenty minutes trying to work a knife through the plastic seal around the door to see if there is any light inside.

'Maybe you could sit inside while I close it,' suggests Ruby, but the fridge is too small to sit inside. It looks like we will never know.

I notice something strange about the fridge. It is completely empty.

'What happened to our food?'

'I felt disgusted by the act of eating,' Ruby tells me. 'So I threw it all away.'

'You seriously expect divine help in a reconciliation with your old girlfriend when you are so wasteful as to throw away food?' says the Archangel Gamiel, hovering outside the window.

I try to explain that it wasn't me, but he doesn't seem interested.

There is a knock on the door. It is a neighbour asking us if we would like to open some cans of cat food for her. She acts like we should be pleased.

We lend them our can-opener but we are still a little puzzled as to why they should come to us.

'Maybe their can-opener broke.'

Broke again, I ask Ruby to phone up the industrial agency for me and she finds me a job as a temporary labourer in Kennington.

Before leaving for work I make Ruby promise to take

good care of our cacti. Ruby says she will but she also says she no longer thinks that her relationship with Domino will turn out well, no matter what the cactus does. But I still have faith. When I am in the flat I check every half hour for the start of a flower.

As soon as I walk onto the site in Kennington they give me a pneumatic drill and tell me to help level out the rocky earth.

I have never used a drill before and it keeps jumping around and threatening to cut off my toes. I do the best I can and no one seems to mind that my progress is very slow. In the earth I am levelling there are a few small yellow flowers. I hate killing them. If all plants are friends then my cactus will be annoyed at me.

It starts to rain and I keep on drilling. After a few minutes I notice that everyone else has taken shelter under the roof of the labourers' hut.

At lunchtime I try and make conversation by asking if anyone knows any good drummers looking for a band, but no one does. I am so obviously ignorant of what to do on a building site that no one takes much notice of me.

When we have levelled out the site we have to clear everything away in wheelbarrows. The rubbish tip is across a deep ditch and to get there I have to struggle my wheelbarrow uphill across a sloping and shaky plank of wood. Each time I do this I almost fall in the ditch and if I fall in the ditch the wheelbarrow full of rubble will come down on top of me.

I'm scared of this, Cis, I say in my head.

No one else has any problems doing this and, struggling over, I feel increasingly stupid and incompetent. At the end of the day the foreman tells me that tomorrow there is not so much work on so I need not come back.

'I am a poor labourer,' I tell Ruby.

'At least you got one day's wages,' she says, comfortingly, and afterwards she runs me a bath and washes the building-site filth out of my hair and massages my shoulders. When I go down to the agency's offices to pick up my money they give me two days' wages by mistake.

Ruby tells me that Daita the Vietnamese Tree Goddess is also the Friend of Poor Labourers everywhere and probably she is responsible for my extra day's wage so I buy some incense and light a stick for her. I also buy Ruby some more new sunglasses and some nail-varnish. She is very pleased at this and brings home a boy to fuck who is not Domino. This is unusual but not unheard of.

I wonder if she is managing with her diaphragm.

Lying in bed I can hear them fucking.

Bandits enter through my open window. Bad advice from the police. They kidnap me and try to carry me off but I escape and hide on a council estate till they have gone. I hide in a stairwell along with a lonely cat and a ripped plastic bag full of flowers and beer cans.

When I am safe from the bandits I wander over to Cis's sister's flat. It is on the third floor. I stare through the window.

'Help me with my diaphragm,' says Ruby. 'It keeps coming out.'

'Are you sure it's the right size?'

'The doctor measured me.'

I put it in for her. On her vagina I can smell the breath of her lover.

Cis is visiting her sister. With her is her new boyfriend. I notice that he is not all that good-looking. But he is good company and they are having fun discussing an old wreck of a motorbike that they're going to try fixing up together.

Moans come from Ruby's room. Sometimes she makes a lot of noise when she is fucking. I am glad she is not with Domino. I hate Domino.

Next morning I make them some tea.

'Last night I dreamed I was kidnapped by bandits,' says Ruby. 'But I escaped and hid on a council estate.'

'How is your orgasmic response?'

'Much better. I am going to write it an appreciative letter.'

Her new lover plays drums and I ask him to play in my band.

Cynthia, sick, howls at the moon again

Cynthia, weak from loss of blood after her battle with Lupus, limps along in the freezing rain through a miserable south London street where all the shops are boarded up and all the boards are covered with cheap posters advertising last month's meetings and last week's gigs. Fevered, she hallucinates that Paris is selling fruit from a market stall. He is with another girl, holding her hand and smiling into her eyes.

Behind the next block is her rubbish tip. She lies down on it and contemplates her life: no friends, no family and her mother dead; betrayed by Uncle Bartholomew; worst of all, her soul still trapped by a man who doesn't love her. And she's lost her guitar again.

Unable to think of anything better to do, she starts to howl at the moon.

'What is that terrible noise?' asks a young woman, picking her way over the rubbish tip.

'It is me, Cynthia Werewolf, howling at the moon. Go away or I'll eat you.'

'You're too weak to eat anyone.'

'Who are you?'

'I'm Ruby Werewolf – pirate, slayer, thief, reaver, painter, poet, writer, artist and uncontrollable adventurer.'

'Pleased to meet you,' says Cynthia, impressed.

A necklace glints at the throat of the stranger. It is Cynthia's werewolf soul necklace.

'Where did you get that?' she demands.

'A man gave it to me,' replies Ruby. 'He said he loved me but most days he doesn't seem too sure about it. I've been at home all week but he hasn't called round.'

'You don't really sound like much of an adventurer,' comments Cynthia.

'I'm having a short holiday.'

*Cynthia passes out and Ruby helps her home and bathes
her wounds.*

~

All Autumn I carried on being mainly unemployed with a
few days' work here and there, looking forward to finally
getting my gig organised, and thinking about Cis. I wondered what she was doing. I had no doubt that whatever
Cis was doing she was particularly happy doing it, although
it was raining all the time, and I remembered that Cis did
not like the rain.

Trudging around on the blackened plain, the robot gives
me a print-out saying it has an important piece of news for
me. However, I am at that moment late for work and I
can't wait around to hear it.

I am working in a carpet warehouse in Hackney, loading
rolls of carpet onto trucks. This job lasts for three days and
during it one of the other people employed there seriously
hurts his back lifting a heavy carpet and has to go home in
a taxi.

Izzy, expert on weights, has told me to be careful with
my back when lifting things. I manage not to hurt myself,
but it is no fun loading all the trucks.

The other workers are slightly jealous of the men who

drive these trucks. We imagine that driving a truck must be easier and more lucrative than loading them. I expect it has its problems as well.

When the warehouse is emptied the job comes to an end.

'OK robot,' I ask, 'what was this important piece of news?'

But the robot has disappeared. It is nowhere in sight. I hunt over the blackened plains of three continents but I never find it again. I miss the robot. It was not much of a companion but there is no one else for me to talk to.

Ruby is in a slightly bad mood because Domino has been being particularly unfriendly, claiming that he is too busy to see her this week.

She tells me that she has utterly given up on him. She is lying of course, and when we go to a party and she meets someone who she thinks might possibly be having some sort of relationship with him she is very displeased.

Depressed, she lies around doing not very much. The contact article seems to have been forgotten about. Occasionally she gets drunk and plans out more werewolf stories, although she is actually in a bad mood with her werewolf story as well, because Domino asked her if there was something Freudian in all this talk of werewolves eating their lovers. Ruby was outraged at this, telling me crossly that Freud was a notorious moron with ridiculous theories about female sexuality, quite apart from the fact that Domino couldn't tell Freud from a carrot cake if his life depended on it, in fact Domino couldn't do anything whatsoever if his life depended on it, except drink beer and talk loudly all the time and make sure his hair was looking good.

'I'm depressed in here,' says Ruby. 'Let's go visit Izzy and Marilyn.'

I'm surprised at Ruby wanting to leave the house.

'It's raining.'

'Well, we'll take an umbrella,' she says.

Ruby sees that I am not enthusiastic.

'Come on,' she says. 'We might meet Cis in the street. You know she used to like being out in the rain.'

Izzy and Marilyn are not home so we sit in a café instead and drink cups of tea and have a good bout of self-pity, with Ruby telling me what a terrible life it is when you are constantly messed around by your lover and me telling her much the same thing. Ruby is frustrated because she knows someone who will buy chequebooks and cheque cards from us at ten pounds a cheque which would be a hundred and fifty pounds if the chequebook was full, but we do not know anyone with a chequebook and cheque card. Even petty fraud can be difficult to make a good start in. I am distracted during this conversation because Cis walks past the window of the café at least fifteen times while we are sitting there, but no matter how hard I try to catch her eye, she never looks in.

Cynthia regains her health and leads a quiet life for a while

Ruby makes Cynthia nourishing soup and nurses her back to health. They become friends immediately, neither of them ever having met a werewolf before who they really liked – apart from Uncle Bartholomew, and even he turned out badly in the end.

A strange coincidence, muses Cynthia, that we should both be sad over the same man.

'I've brought you some new clothes,' says Ruby. 'And a few newspapers in case you get bored while I'm pirating and adventuring.'

'Thank you. But I don't need the shoes. I never wear any shoes.'

'Neither do I. What are you going to do when you are better?'

Cynthia shrugs.

'I have no idea. My life is empty and meaningless.'

As Ruby Werewolf, despite her claims, is not really doing much adventuring right now, they spend the evenings together decorating Ruby's room with black walls and bright pictures.

After a while, Cynthia decides she should move on. She doesn't have to, now that she is safe from the detectives, but being in any one place for too long depresses her.

Before she leaves, Ruby gives her back the necklace, because Ruby has utterly given up on Paris.

~

On the day my cactus flowers I am offered a job in Brixton dole office. If there is a connection here I can't see it. The cactus grows a wonderful flower, radiant yellow, a little desert oasis in my damp bedroom.

In the dole office I have to take fresh claims, people signing on for the first time or people signing on after finishing work.

I do not want to work here but as one of the criteria for signing on is that I am available for employment, I cannot refuse the offer. At least it is only temporary. Another of the clerks in my section knows Cis and sometimes he tells me news about her.

Izzy and Marilyn have to move house when their short-life tenancy comes to an end. They move into a new squat with three other people because they cannot find anywhere decent otherwise.

Ruby visits them and later she tells me that it is a nice place and Izzy is still lifting her weights, without any visible results.

'But it keeps her happy. I told her they should ask Tilka the Goddess of Squatters to look after them, but they didn't seem to think it was necessary.'

John, Ruby's new lover, is a good drummer and easy to get on with. He joins the band and we organise our gig.

'My cactus has bloomed. When will Cis knock at the door?'

'Any day,' says Ruby. 'Of course she might just wait till

your gig. Probably she will want to see you onstage. Make us some tea.'

'Do you want to eat? I bought a bag full of healthy Stone Age things.'

Ruby shakes her head.

'Eating disgusts me.'

She must feel bad about Domino. She is still sleeping with John the drummer.

We are evicted and move to a squat in Bengeworth Road. There is no electricity and we find out after we've moved that it is disconnected in a way that means we cannot put it back on. By coincidence Bengeworth Road is the site of the main electricity offices in Brixton.

'Strange,' says Ruby, in the gloom. 'They have plenty of electricity up there but they won't give us any. I'd better find us somewhere else to live.'

I meet Jane who is selling socialist newspapers outside the tube station.

'We can't find anywhere to live.'

'Of course not. The government won't provide houses for poor people. They don't give local councils any money to build council houses. They are only interested in rich people buying property.'

A strange accusation, it seems to me. Everyone knows that if you can't find somewhere to live it is because you have offended Ixanbarg, the Bad Housing Demon. I'm sure the government is doing its best.

Some people in the government introduce a bill to

restrict abortion rights. Ruby, outraged, decides to join the local campaign against this bill and I join along with her. Every Tuesday we go to a meeting in the Town Hall and every Saturday we hand out leaflets in the street and get people to sign our petition.

I am good in this campaign because I am a reliable person for handing out leaflets and I never try to make any decisions or decide policy.

Ruby is slightly more vocal but I am happier just being told where I have to go and what leaflets I have to hand out.

At the same time the government introduces more legislation which is anti-homosexual and there is a large campaign against this and sometimes our whole pro-abortion group goes on demonstrations for gay rights. I help carry our banner.

My cactus is in full flower and the gig is next week. John finds a PA. I can play all our songs. Ruby stops sleeping with John and finds us a place to live, a council flat that we can stay in for three months till the tenant comes back from her holiday in Vietnam.

'Will we say a prayer to Tilka?' I ask, when all our belongings are moved in.

'Tilka only looks after squatters,' Ruby tells me.

'Who is the god of council tenants?'

'There is no god for council tenants.'

It is December and I hand out leaflets in the snow. Ruby strides through the snow barefoot and still wears her sunglasses and we live on chocolate biscuits and bananas, which is a satisfying diet. I worry about her feet but they seem to be tough enough for any weather conditions. She does put a donkey jacket over her dress, though, and sometimes she has to stop and wipe the snow off her sunglasses.

In the dole office I take hundreds of fresh claims every day and sometimes people ask me when they will get their first Giro because they are desperate for money. I tell them that it will probably be soon even though I know that it won't be. If I don't say this they will shout and argue at me and I am just the lowest clerk and I can't do anything about it. I don't even want to be here.

When anyone needs to find the papers relating to a client they are always missing. The dole office has clerks whose only job is to try and link up missing papers. Sometimes among the long depressing queues there is shouting and scuffling and angry people pleading for money, and when a middle-aged man bursts into tears in front of me because he has forgotten to bring his P45 I start to think that maybe it is all my fault after all.

Cynthia makes a commendable vow, and fails to keep it

Cynthia, free from the worry of pursuit by Lupus, has no idea what to do with herself.

Where oh where is my Paris, she thinks sadly. And will I ever see him again?

Penniless, she eats the new door off the second-hand music shop in Brixton and makes off with another guitar and a portable cassette player. Being a powerful werewolf has its compensations. She gets back to busking and listening to country music. Ruby is very keen on country music.

Cynthia decides to go through the rest of her life never harming anyone.

Cheered by this thought, she strums her guitar as she walks along the street.

Hungry, she is going to use her day's taking from busking to buy a vegetarian pizza.

The full moon shines weakly through the dusk. Cynthia momentarily mistakes a young girl for a pizza and snaps at her throat.

Oh fuck it, she thinks. Another one gone. I will never learn any self-control.

She drags the young girl's body into a small patch of scrubby grass in front of a desolate-looking Army Careers Office. She stares morosely at the dead face for a few minutes, then leaves.

~

In the snow I hand an abortion leaflet to Cis.

'Thank you,' she says. 'I have never seen you do anything useful before.'

Ruby and I have been petitioning for two hours and we are frozen.

Izzy sees us in the street and she signs our petition and then brings us some pizza from the market and cups of coffee in polystyrene beakers.

'I do not feel the cold so much anymore,' she says, 'because I am more muscular than I used to be. Do you want to see my biceps?'

'Not right now,' says Ruby, a little harshly.

'We were all arrested yesterday,' Izzy tells us. 'The police broke down the door of our new squat and took us to the police station. They kept us in overnight. We've been charged with stealing electricity and they've boarded up the house.'

We sympathise with Izzy. She is having a hard time.

Back home Ruby puts her feet in my lap to warm them. I massage her toes and rub her calves till the blood starts to flow again.

We have chocolate biscuits and bananas and with my wages from the dole office we are well off for a while.

Every day Cis and her new boyfriend drive past the window on their new motorbike, but I am not worried anymore now that my cactus has flowered.

The cold weather makes my knee hurt. My knee is damaged and badly scarred from an inglorious motorbike accident. I fell off when I was learning to ride it. The scar looks like it has been sewed up with a fish-hook.

'I think your stories are getting worse,' says Ruby.

'What stories?'

'The ones where you are trapped on a foreign planet.

The ones where you say you are resigned to walking round with a stupid robot and never having fun anymore.'

'Ruby, I never told you any story like that.'

'Yes you did and it is a very obvious image. You'll have to start either living in the real world or writing better stories.'

Ruby is slightly upset. I know why. Last week I could not get into work because I was waylaid by a pack of snow-wolves in Coldharbour Lane. When I went home Ruby had been crying because she had seen Domino walking along with another woman. Now she won't eat.

If any of Ruby's friends stopped eating and acted sad because of a fool like Domino, Ruby would give them a severe talking to.

I apologise to my supervisor about not coming in to work and tell her that I could not get past the pack of snow-wolves.

'Werewolves? In Brixton?'

'Not werewolves. Snow-wolves.'

While I am working in the dole office the old woman who sits on the balcony throws a little party. She invites Ascanazl, Spirit Friend of Lonely People, Shamash the Sun God, Tilka the Goddess of Squatters, Jasmine the Divine Protectress of Broken Hearts, Daita, Vietnamese Tree Goddess and Friend of Poor Labourers everywhere, and a few others.

They have a good time together. Helena, Goddess of Electric Guitarists, turns up. She is still upset about her girlfriend leaving her and Jasmine does her best to cheer her up. Helena tells everyone that she is keeping herself busy so as to not think about her personal problems. She has started lifting weights to improve her body and she has helped my band organise our gig at last.

'Good,' says Daita. 'He needs some help, he is having a hard time. Last month I got him two days' wages for only one day's work.'

'Good party,' says Ascanazl. 'Any more wine?'

The day after I make the excuse about snow-wolves making me late for work my supervisor tells me that I will not be taken on as a permanent clerk at the dole office. This is such good news I feel like partying.

One time I went to a sauna party where everyone took off their clothes and had saunas, then draped themselves in towels and drank wine. But on the wasted planet there are no good parties. There is not even anyone to talk to, now the robot has disappeared.

People hammer on the door of the dole office but the door won't open. We are on strike because one of the union representatives has been victimised.

I hand out leaflets telling people what the strike is about. Many policemen come down to watch over our picket and they make most of us stand on the patch of grass on the other side of the road. One superintendent is particularly unfriendly and he tells us that anyone who even says the word scab will be arrested and charged with threatening behaviour.

This strike covers my last few days at the dole office and I had already booked these last few days as holiday, so I get paid while everyone else doesn't. I offer to give all my pay to the strike fund but the union representative says I should not because now I am unemployed again and will need the money myself. I keep my wages but I always feel guilty about it.

The abortion bill is defeated so our campaign is a success and Ruby says that Domino is going to meet her at the gig tomorrow and this makes her happy. I am also happy. My cactus is in full flower. Cis is going to come and see me play my new song about her.

'Things are looking good,' I say to Ruby.

It is bitterly cold outside and we have wrapped ourselves in one quilt in front of the fire to keep warm.

'Yes,' she says. 'They always get better in time.'

Ruby says that being wrapped up in a quilt like this reminds her of being a child. I see what she means, although I have no memories of being a child. Ruby claims that she can remember sitting in her pram but, no matter how I try, I cannot recall anything at all before I was sixteen.

Cynthia does not find happiness

Cynthia buys some flowers and takes them to the nearest graveyard. She distributes them randomly on the graves. This is her penance for killing so many innocent people.

Sat down by the walls of the graveyard are five men, very shabby, very thirsty for some wine from the communal bottle. Their fingers are yellowed with nicotine and their trousers are filthy brown with excrement.

The sight of their poverty depresses the young werewolf. Outside there are more derelicts hanging round aimlessly, waiting for the day to pass, begging money for drink and something to eat. Everywhere she looks there seems to be some poor person unable to cope with living. And even the prosperous passers-by don't seem to be very happy.

An ambulance wails its way past, trying to hurry but caught up in heavy traffic. Cynthia imagines that inside there is some person trying to fight off death, and losing.

This is terrible, she thinks. Everything appears to be totally hopeless. I wonder where Paris is? I wonder why he let me down. All this successfully not eating anyone and not being pursued by any assailants has plunged Cynthia depressingly into the real world. She has no friends, her heart aches over Paris, and she is poor all the time.

Sometimes whole days pass without her exchanging a word with another living being, so that even a shop assistant saying a cheery hello to her seems like a happy event.

She buys a newspaper every day. Occasionally she reads the lonely hearts column, but has too much sense to think you could ever fall in love through a contact advert.

Every day she goes for a long walk. Always she hopes to run into Paris, but she never does. The old vicarage he was

*living in is long since boarded-up, and she has no idea where
he might be.*

*'What a life,' she mutters, trying to work her fingers round
a difficult new chord. There is no happiness anywhere. It is a
lousy world, in every respect. I will never see Paris again. I
will never have any friends. I will always be poor and hungry.
It would have been better if I had never been born, and if I
had to be born, I wish I had never fallen in love, because being
in love is a worse curse than being born a werewolf.*

*She fingers her werewolf soul jewel, which she will never
ever give to anyone else, and stares at the moon and howls for
a while. But soon she gets tired even of howling, and tired of
playing guitar, and tired of everything in the whole world, so
she just sits and looks blankly in front of her, and wonders
how long the average lifespan of a werewolf is, and if she
might get lucky and die young.*

～

'Well?' says Ruby. 'What d'you think?'

'I like it. What happens next?'

'Nothing happens next. That's the end.'

I am shocked.

'It can't be. Where is the happy ending?'

Ruby says she doesn't believe in happy endings. I feel
a huge depression creeping towards me.

'Make a happy ending,' I say, slightly desperate. 'I'll be
depressed if Cynthia just sits there being sad for the rest
of her life.'

Ruby, however, will not relent, and there is no happy ending for Cynthia Werewolf.

I dream about the old woman who I used to see on the balcony. I dream she is a goddess. She stands before me in the most resplendent jewelled robe that has ever been woven and tells me to stop being stupid and moaning and whining all the time about my girlfriend leaving me.

Then she advises me not to do any more thirteen-hour night-shifts because it will be terrible for my health and I'm not getting any younger. She wishes me good luck for my gig.

On the day of the gig it rains. This week has been continually wet and none of our posters are still on display. Those ones that haven't slid off the walls or been ripped off the bus shelters have been covered by other posters advertising the meetings of the ever-active local revolutionary parties.

Our friend Matthew arrives with the van and we load up, slightly anxious as always about carrying our instruments off the council estate, anxious as well that nothing should get wet.

Ruby comes with us in the van and we arrive at the pub at six o'clock to wait for the PA to arrive.

'Ruby, why do all these goddesses you tell me about wear flowing robes? Why don't they wear trousers or dungarees?'

'I haven't been telling you about any goddesses.'

'Haven't you?'

'No.'

I'm sure someone has.

'Is Izzy coming tonight?'

'I'm not sure. She told me yesterday she was depressed about being evicted and arrested and her parents nagging her and Dean moaning at her.'

The PA is three minutes late which is three minutes of terrible anxiety. When it arrives I have to pay forty pounds.

The God of Sound Engineers is called Manis. He is a very clever god, always fixing things, but he is also avaricious.

'Hey,' says Izzy, striding through the door. 'You want a hand in with your equipment?'

She takes off her leather jacket and flings it in a corner. The sound man stops connecting leads and stares at her. She is wearing a small vest and underneath her arms ripple with strength. She is burning with health and energy. Her shoulders are sculpted like an artist's illustration of the perfect anatomy. Ruby and I are awestruck. Beside her we are as weak and sickly as broken twigs.

'How are Dean and the parents?' I ask, outside at the van.

'Who cares?' says Izzy, hoisting the mixing desk over her shoulder. 'Who needs them?'

We help carry all the equipment in, large speakers, a

mixing desk, monitors, reels of wire, microphones, more stuff than we really need.

It takes an hour to set up and meanwhile the support band arrives to do their sound-check.

Ruby is on her own in the bar next door.

'Where's Domino?'

She shrugs. 'He hasn't turned up.'

We share a drink and I look outside for any sign of an audience, but all there is is rain.

'Don't worry,' says Ruby, passing me our drink. 'It's early yet.'

We lock one door and set up a table to collect money at the other and Ruby brings in an ashtray to keep it in. She has a rubber stamp to stamp people's hands once they've paid.

'Dear Helena, Goddess of Electric Guitarists. Please protect me from guitar thieves. Please do not let me forget any of our songs. Please prevent me from breaking a string, particularly in the first number. Please don't let the lead come out of my guitar when I dance onstage. Please don't let my fuzzbox become disconnected from my amplifier. Don't let my amplifier stop working again. Don't let Nigel cover up everything I'm playing because he has a better amplifier than me. Please distract everyone's attention when I play some wrong notes. Good luck with your girlfriend.'

Nigel puts the lights down and gives a tape to the sound man to try and create some atmosphere in the empty room.

Me and Nigel and John sit in a corner, making ourselves ready. Ruby sits at the door on her own, trying not
to be sad that Domino has not turned up.

I am nervous. Cis might be here. I told her sister about
the gig.

Some spacemen appear for a second but they disappear
without talking to me. I haven't talked to any spacemen
since my cactus flowered.

I look around, and I realise for the first time what a
drab room this is. Drab and lifeless and totally dull. Too
dull for anyone to enjoy themselves in.

When the support band plays there is an audience of
five. We wait as long as we can before going on in case
more people turn up, but when we start playing there are
eight people watching us.

In the other bar there are many people but they are not
interested in coming in to watch us play.

During our set five more people come in and two
leave. That makes an audience of eleven. All eleven clap.

After a while I forget about my nerves. We finish our
set and the eleven people drift away.

We help the PA people out with their equipment. I
have to give them another forty pounds, so on the night
we have lost fifty-four pounds, and another ten for the
posters plus five pounds to Matthew for driving us.

Izzy wishes us a cheery goodbye and strides away confidently into the night, a very powerful presence. Every
eye follows her as she leaves.

As a gig it is a total failure and I am completely depressed. So are Nigel and John. We are all silent as Matthew drops us home.

Enough human suffering

Enough human suffering, I think, wandering aimlessly round my room. I hunt out some paper and a pencil.

Cynthia Werewolf places an advert for musicians in a music paper. She is surprisingly successful with this advert because werewolves sometimes do get lucky breaks. A guitarist she likes answers right away and he knows a good bass guitarist. They have no trouble at all in finding a drummer, in fact they have several to choose from.

They practise downstairs in the basement of a squat and soon Cynthia's demented love-crazed genius begins to produce powerful results. They develop into the most violently beautiful country punk band ever to see the light of day, sounding somewhere between Extreme Noise Terror and Loretta Lynn.

Soon they are playing local gigs and making a name for themselves. Cynthia, verging on success, has friends and admirers everywhere. Almost happy, she no longer feels the urge to rip people apart and eat them, even on the brightest of full moons. Standing onstage, singing and playing, with feedback whining all around and her Stetson perched on top of her head, she is as contented as she has ever been. When the band play the song she has written about Paris the audience riot in appreciation.

Only her lingering heartache over Paris prevents her from being completely satisfied. But while in the real world lovers never return, and stories about people who go out and win back their lovers are all lies, Cynthia, being a mythical being, is not strictly bound by these rules.

One night, after a gig in which representatives from several record companies are seen enjoying themselves in the audience, Paris walks into the dressing room.

'I heard your song about me,' he tells her. 'It was wonderful. I realise now that I have always loved you. Please take me back.'

Cynthia is overjoyed. Really she should hate Paris for all the misery he has caused her, and certainly she should at least give him a hard time about the whole thing, but she is in fact too happy to bother. She embraces him passionately, and takes him home.

Back in her flat she slips the soul necklace round his neck again and they go to bed. They fuck for hours on end. Paris is still not all that good a lover, but Cynthia knows she can improve things, given time.

And ever afterwards, Cynthia and Paris are famous for being a happy couple, immune to the stupidity and misery of the world around them. The band goes from strength to strength, and Cynthia is never ever lonely again.

~

'What do you think?' I ask Ruby. She says she doesn't really think much of it, but she doesn't mind if it makes me happy. It seems like a big improvement to me.

'We have lost sixty-nine pounds,' I say, back in the flat.

'Never mind,' says Ruby. 'I'll think of some way to get money.'

We have a long silence.

'Cis never came.'

'There wasn't any chance she would.'

'I know. But I would have liked her to hear my song.'

Ruby makes me some tea.

'My life has seemed strange recently.'

Ruby says she has noticed.

'You remember you said you always feel better in time?'

'Yes.'

'I feel worse.'

'That can happen as well.'

Right.

Ruby shrugs. I am empty-headed. My whole body is hollow and without feeling. No, I am lying. There are little bits here that don't feel too good. I imagine that Ruby is feeling immense pain inside about Domino, messing her around all the time. I'm not entirely sure if she is. I do not know if it is really possible to know what anyone else is feeling. Maybe she is just hollow as well.

'Ruby, could you tell me something optimistic and cheerful before I go to bed?'

'My knee is feeling better.'

'So is mine.'

I am a little cheered.

'And we are good friends,' says Ruby, smiling.

'Yes. You are the best friend I ever had.'

'Do you remember the can-opener? And all those beans?'

We start to laugh. We laugh and laugh till Ruby starts to roll on the floor and complain about her sides hurting. We laugh about nothing till we are completely worn out.

Then we kiss and go to bed. Ruby has the best bedroom, because she got here first, but I would have let her have it anyway. A friend like Ruby is hard to find.

My cactus thrives although Ruby's never flowers. Despite this she later moves out to live with Domino. After a while they have a terminal argument and she goes back to live with her parents. We lose touch.

I find a job as a library assistant in a college and I am quite well suited to this, sitting quietly behind a counter stamping books, watching the students. Without Ruby's support I stop squatting and start paying rent. I miss Ruby terribly. And I miss the spaceman and Tilka and Ascanazl and the flowers and the old woman who is never on the balcony anymore and the mad schemes for making money and the robots and the art class and everything else. Most of all I miss Cis. I see her sometimes walking in the street and sometimes on her bicycle, but I never talk to her.

LONELY WEREWOLF GIRL

As teenage werewolf Kalix MacRinnalch is pursued through the streets of London by murderous hunters, her sister, the Werewolf Enchantress, is busy designing clothes for the Fire Queen. Meanwhile, in the Scottish Highlands, the MacRinnalch Clan is plotting and feuding after the head of the clan suddenly dies intestate.

As court intrigue threatens to explode in all-out civil war, the competing factions determine that Kalix is the swing vote necessary to assume leadership of the clan. Unfortunately, Kalix isn't really into clan politics – laudanum's more her thing. But what's even more unfortunate is that Kalix is the reason the head of the clan ended up dead, which is why she's now on the run in London . . .

978-0-7499-4283-0

CURSE OF THE WOLF GIRL

Scottish teenage werewolf Kalix MacRinnalch is in London trying to settle down and live a normal life. Her new friends support her as she goes to college to learn to read and write, but her old enemies won't leave her alone. Many powerful werewolves want Kalix dead, and the Guild of Werewolf Hunters is still dedicated to wiping out the entire MacRinnalch werewolf clan.

Life might be easier if Kalix's family were able to help, but her sister the Enchantress needs all of her powers to locate the perfect pair of high heels, her brother Markus is busy in Scotland organising an opera, and her cousin Dominil is engaged in her own merciless vendetta. Kalix must carry on alone but she's finding it difficult enough to pay the rent without having to deal with werewolf hunters and exams at the same time . . .

978-0-7499-4288-5

Do you love fiction with a supernatural twist?

Want the chance to hear news about your favourite authors (and the chance to win free books)?

Keri Arthur
S. G. Browne
P.C. Cast
Christine Feehan
Jacquelyn Frank
Thea Harrison
Larissa Ione
Darynda Jones
Sherrilyn Kenyon
Jackie Kessler
Jayne Ann Krentz and Jayne Castle
Martin Millar
Kat Richardson
J.R. Ward
David Wellington
Laura Wright

Then visit the Piatkus website and blog
www.piatkus.co.uk | www.piatkusbooks.net

And follow us on Facebook and Twitter
www.facebook.com/piatkusfiction | www.twitter.com/piatkusbooks